TO PUNISH THEM

DI SAM COBBS

BOOK SIX

M A COMLEY

COPYRIGHT

For Alpha, now dearly departed.
Clive, I hope you enjoy many new adventures with Jet.
Thank you for supplying yet another stunning photo to use as a cover.
M xx

ACKNOWLEDGMENTS

Special thanks as always go to @studioenp for their superb cover design expertise.

My heartfelt thanks go to my wonderful editor Emmy, and my proofreaders Joseph and Barbara for spotting all the lingering nits.

Thank you also to my amazing ARC Group who help to keep me sane during this process.

To Mary, gone, but never forgotten. I hope you found the peace you were searching for my dear friend. I miss you each and every day.

ALSO BY M A COMLEY

Blind Justice (Novella)

Cruel Justice (Book #1)

Mortal Justice (Novella)

Impeding Justice (Book #2)

Final Justice (Book #3)

Foul Justice (Book #4)

Guaranteed Justice (Book #5)

Ultimate Justice (Book #6)

Virtual Justice (Book #7)

Hostile Justice (Book #8)

Tortured Justice (Book #9)

Rough Justice (Book #10)

Dubious Justice (Book #11)

Calculated Justice (Book #12)

Twisted Justice (Book #13)

Justice at Christmas (Short Story)

Prime Justice (Book #14)

Heroic Justice (Book #15)

Shameful Justice (Book #16)

Immoral Justice (Book #17)

Toxic Justice (Book #18)

Overdue Justice (Book #19)

Unfair Justice (a 10,000 word short story)

Irrational Justice (a 10,000 word short story)

Seeking Justice (a 15,000 word novella)
Caring For Justice (a 24,000 word novella)
Savage Justice (a 17,000 word novella)
Justice at Christmas #2 (a 15,000 word novella)
Gone in Seconds (Justice Again series #1)
Ultimate Dilemma (Justice Again series #2)
Shot of Silence (Justice Again series #3)
Taste of Fury (Justice Again series #4)
Crying Shame (Justice Again series #5)
To Die For (DI Sam Cobbs #1)
To Silence Them (DI Sam Cobbs #2)
To Make Them Pay (DI Sam Cobbs #3)
To Prove Fatal (DI Sam Cobbs #4)
To Condemn Them (DI Sam Cobbs #5)
To Punish Them (DI Sam Cobbs #6)
To Entice Them (DI Sam Cobbs #7)
Forever Watching You (DI Miranda Carr thriller)
Wrong Place (DI Sally Parker thriller #1)
No Hiding Place (DI Sally Parker thriller #2)
Cold Case (DI Sally Parker thriller#3)
Deadly Encounter (DI Sally Parker thriller #4)
Lost Innocence (DI Sally Parker thriller #5)
Goodbye My Precious Child (DI Sally Parker #6)
The Missing Wife (DI Sally Parker #7)
Truth or Dare (DI Sally Parker #8)
Web of Deceit (DI Sally Parker Novella with Tara Lyons)
The Missing Children (DI Kayli Bright #1)
Killer On The Run (DI Kayli Bright #2)

Hidden Agenda (DI Kayli Bright #3)

Murderous Betrayal (Kayli Bright #4)

Dying Breath (Kayli Bright #5)

Taken (DI Kayli Bright #6)

The Hostage Takers (DI Kayli Bright Novella)

No Right to Kill (DI Sara Ramsey #1)

Killer Blow (DI Sara Ramsey #2)

The Dead Can't Speak (DI Sara Ramsey #3)

Deluded (DI Sara Ramsey #4)

The Murder Pact (DI Sara Ramsey #5)

Twisted Revenge (DI Sara Ramsey #6)

The Lies She Told (DI Sara Ramsey #7)

For The Love Of… (DI Sara Ramsey #8)

Run for Your Life (DI Sara Ramsey #9)

Cold Mercy (DI Sara Ramsey #10)

Sign of Evil (DI Sara Ramsey #11)

Indefensible (DI Sara Ramsey #12)

Locked Away (DI Sara Ramsey #13)

I Can See You (DI Sara Ramsey #14)

The Kill List (DI Sara Ramsey #15)

Crossing The Line (DI Sara Ramsey #16)

Time to Kill (DI Sara Ramsey #17)

Deadly Passion (DI Sara Ramsey #18)

I Know The Truth (A Psychological thriller)

She's Gone (A psychological thriller)

Shattered Lives (A psychological thriller)

Evil In Disguise – a novel based on True events

Deadly Act (Hero series novella)

Torn Apart (Hero series #1)

End Result (Hero series #2)

In Plain Sight (Hero Series #3)

Double Jeopardy (Hero Series #4)

Criminal Actions (Hero Series #5)

Regrets Mean Nothing (Hero series #6)

Prowlers (Di Hero Series #7)

Sole Intention (Intention series #1)

Grave Intention (Intention series #2)

Devious Intention (Intention #3)

Cozy mysteries

Murder at the Wedding

Murder at the Hotel

Murder by the Sea

Death on the Coast

Death By Association

Merry Widow (A Lorne Simpkins short story)

It's A Dog's Life (A Lorne Simpkins short story)

A Time To Heal (A Sweet Romance)

A Time For Change (A Sweet Romance)

High Spirits

The Temptation series (Romantic Suspense/New Adult Novellas)

Past Temptation

Lost Temptation

Clever Deception (co-written by Linda S Prather)

Tragic Deception (co-written by Linda S Prather)

Sinful Deception (co-written by Linda S Prather)

PROLOGUE

Fern listened to the tall tale her friend, Justine, was telling her, smiling broadly. She sipped at her orange juice and nodded. "That would do it for me. If Wayne ever tried to pull the wool over my eyes with those words, I'd be out the door, no messing. Life's too short to put up with such antics from your partner."

"Oh, yeah, so you say. What about the time he told you he was going away on a teacher's conference and two days later you found lipstick stains on his collar? Or have you conveniently forgotten all about that incident?" Justine wagged her finger from side to side like a metronome.

"Ugh, yeah, I'd forgotten that particular episode."

"Selective memory, that's what you've got, my girl. You sit there, week after week, dishing out your well-meaning advice to all and sundry, but when it comes to dealing with Wayne, it's a whole different ball game, isn't it?" Justine took a sip from her white wine and soda and folded her arms.

Fern twisted her mouth and pulled a face at the woman she'd considered to be her best friend since the day they had joined secondary school together.

The others laughed.

"You two, you're always having a bloody dig at each other about your respective partners. Give it a rest for a change before things escalate and bite you in the arse," Lisa warned.

"I'm done handing out advice which is ultimately ignored," Fern replied.

"It's not," Justine mumbled.

"Leave it, the pair of you," Mandy advised.

After that fractious exchange, the four of them stuck to relatively safer topics of conversation, mainly to do with work. They were all teachers at the same primary school in the centre of Workington. They'd been friends for years, not as long as Justine and Fern, granted, but good friends, nevertheless.

"What about Sid, is he going to live up to his promise and whisk you away this weekend, Lisa?" Fern asked.

"There's still talk of that happening. I'm not holding my breath, though. He's always coming up with a plan for this, that and the other, but it never seems to come to fruition," Lisa retorted, her tone as downbeat as her expression.

"Why put up with that, Lis?" Justine demanded, never one to hold back when there was something bugging her.

Lisa's cheeks glowed. "Because I love him. He might be a wrong 'un in your eyes, ladies, but most of the time he treats me well."

"You deserve better than that," Fern muttered. She took a sip from her orange juice and continued, "How many chances are you going to give him?"

Lisa sighed and shook her head. "Can we not make this a 'have a go at how useless Sid is' kind of conversation? We all know every man has his faults in the eyes of our friends, none of them are perfect. Let's face it, neither are we."

Fern covered Lisa's hand with her own and squeezed. "Sorry, you're right. I'll back away now before I say something I might regret. I'd better be making a move. I promised Wayne I would cook him his favourite meal tonight, and it's going to take me at least an hour to prepare when I get home."

"You're crazy, and on a school night, too. Postpone it until the weekend. Can't you come up with an excuse that you have exam papers to mark, like he does—all too frequently in my opinion?"

They all laughed.

"Hardly, since when can a primary school teacher call on that one to be in her arsenal? It's fine, I don't mind, not really. I find standing over a hot stove somewhat therapeutic midweek."

Lisa's cheeks billowed. "Rather you than me. All I ever do is go home and use my finger to dial for a takeaway." She patted her rounded stomach and shrugged. "I know I shouldn't, but when Wednesday comes around, I'm all out of ideas and my enthusiasm has wavered considerably, so spending hours in the kitchen just seems like yet another grim domestic chore I can do without."

Fern tutted. "You're unbelievable. There's only one person who has benefited from you getting married six months ago, and it's *not* that wonderful husband of yours, it's the guy running the pizza place at the end of your road."

Lisa pointed at Fern. "Ha, you're just jealous."

"I don't think so. Remind me, how many stones have you put on since you tied the knot with Sid?"

Lisa sucked in a breath and placed a hand over her heart. "Ouch! That one cut deep, too deep. Take it back, you evil woman."

Fern chuckled. "I bloody won't. All you do is bend our ear for hours on end about what the scales are shouting every week and yet you're unwilling to do anything about it and, if anything, are intent on making your scales groan even more under your weight. Anyway, I'm all done lecturing you tonight, I have to be on my way. Enjoy the rest of your evening, ladies. I'll see you bright and early at school in the morning. Don't forget we're stopping behind for a brief meeting with Mrs O'Connell tomorrow. She's determined to get the school nativity plans perfected early this year."

"It's not even the end of October, does she realise that?" Justine asked.

"She does, but she's on holiday at the beginning of November and wants it all done and dusted by then," Fern said.

"Charming, that is, to have a holiday during term time. How many of us can get away with that?" Lisa huffed.

"Special circumstances. Her son is getting married out in America, so we're going to have to suck it up and hope we manage okay without her while she's away," Fern stated.

Justine groaned and hissed, "It's all right for some. Definitely a case of one rule for one and one for the rest of us."

Fern removed the strap of her handbag from the back of her chair, downed the rest of her OJ and stood. "I refuse to get involved in the rights and wrongs of this debate. There's nowt we can do about it, ladies, we have to accept it for what it is: the head rejoicing in the fact that her thirty-five-year-old son is finally getting hitched."

"I pity the woman he's marrying," Lisa voiced unkindly.

Fern blew them all a kiss and waved farewell. She trotted out of the pub and made her way across the car park to her Audi. Her head was down, her mind running through the ingredients she would need for the goulash she was about to conjure up. Did she have everything in the pantry? She couldn't recall having the cream she needed to make the sauce. "I'll stop off at the Co-op on the corner on the way home."

"Sorry, did you say something?" A man approached her from the side, startling her.

"What? No, sorry, I'm guilty of talking to myself."

"Ah, yes, my wife used to be the same, before the cancer took her last year."

"Oh, how sad. You have my condolences." She peered closer at the stranger and frowned. "Don't I know you?"

He turned his head and scurried away. "I don't think so. I have to go," he cast over his shoulder, making his escape.

Fern shrugged off the awkward encounter and pressed her key fob. The doors clunked open. She hopped behind the steering wheel and slowly drove towards the exit, but then she noticed the man turn around and head back to his car.

How odd. Maybe he's forgotten something.

Once a gap in the traffic appeared, she pulled onto the main road. It wasn't until she turned the next corner that Fern realised she was being followed. Tentatively, she put her foot down, testing the driver to see if he was tailing her or not. He was. He kept up with her until the lights at the cross-road ahead. With her pulse racing and her stomach muscles contracting, she was unsure what to do for the best. The lights changed. She pressed down heavily on the accelerator and made a right turn at the last minute. The car shot past, outwitted by her smart manoeuvre.

Fern let out a relieved sigh and settled into her seat, relaxing now that any imminent danger had passed. That was, until the same car emerged behind her.

"Shit, I'm sure that's him. He has one of those air fresheners dangling from his rear-view mirror. What the heck does he want from me? I'm going to try and lose him. Not that I was successful last time I tried to outsmart him. What other option do I have open to me?"

The car lunged forward, and her breathing became as erratic as her driving, but still the car came hurtling after her.

She glanced sideways at her handbag and wondered if she had the courage to release her tight grip on the wheel to remove her phone from inside the flap. She didn't, how could she? She was travelling too fast, and the road ahead was winding first one way and then the other, not giving her time to do anything other than concentrate on her speed and her surroundings.

Shit! What did I say to him to make him come after me like this? Crap, please, God, don't let me down now when I need you the most. Stop this man, now!

With that, she inched her foot down harder on the pedal, and the car shot forward. She took the corner faster than she'd anticipated, and the tyres squealed their objection as the car spun one-eighty degrees. She was thrust forward. The impact proving too much for the car not to crunch under the strain, just like her nerves. Fern tried to unclip the seatbelt, but it was jammed.

Help me, I can't get out of this damn thing.

The driver's door was wrenched open, and the man she had spoken to in the pub car park was standing there, grinning down at her.

"Going somewhere?" he asked.

"Look, I don't know what this is about. If I offended you in some way, I'm truly sorry, I never meant to."

"Didn't you? You say that now, faced with adversity, but then, we all know words are cheap most of the time, don't we?"

"No, I never say anything I don't mean. Please, you have to believe me. How… how can I make this up to you?" she asked, detesting the words before they had even left her mouth.

"Hmm… I'll have to think about that. Get out of the car."

She scanned the darkness surrounding her. They were in the middle of nowhere, no streetlights to highlight the accident and no cars flying past she could flag down to help her. "Sorry? What do you want from me?"

"You'll see soon enough. Get out! Now."

"I would if I could, but I can't, the seatbelt is locked into position, there's no way for me to get out of it."

He produced a large penknife, the type people took camping that had a blade for every occasion. She inhaled a breath. The blade inched closer to her midriff. He slashed at the nylon seatbelt, and it still wouldn't shift. His anger mounted at the same rate as her fear hit an extra level. He growled and sawed at the fabric with yet another robust blade. This time, he managed to cut through it, releasing Fern. She feared what was about to happen next. She didn't see it coming until the last second. He thumped her, catching her on the chin. Her head jolted to the right until she saw stars. Everything after that appeared to happen in slow motion. He dragged her from the front seat and then reached into the car to grab her handbag.

"N… o… wait, what… are you… doing?" She kicked out at him, but her coordination was way off the mark, and she slumped against his stomach with a thud.

"Keep still or I'll make you sorry."

"Why? Why are you… doing this?" She wanted to ask so much more but couldn't get her tongue to cooperate well enough.

"Shut the fuck up."

He punched her a second time, and everything went black.

* * *

He bundled her into the boot of his car and secured the lid, then he went to work. He snapped on a pair of gloves and then jumped behind the wheel of her Audi and turned the key in the ignition, grateful the engine sprang to life at the first attempt and that the smash hadn't damaged it too much. He drove up the road a little way to the gate he'd sourced earlier, hopped out of the vehicle, unlatched the gate and eased it into the overgrown field. Then he sprinted back to the car and drove through the opening. He parked alongside the hedgerow so the Audi wouldn't be seen and then closed the gate behind him and returned to his own car.

Grinning that he'd managed to pull off his crazy scheme, he started the engine and drove towards his remote cottage. He had plans for the woman—she wasn't the only one either. The abduction had been cleaner than he'd anticipated. He had an idea that once she woke up, she'd be feistier than she'd been up until now. Only time would tell. He'd need to keep his guard up, just in case.

He approached the country lane that led to his home. The light was on in the lounge, guiding his way. There were no other houses around, no nosey neighbours to contend with. The farmer tended his sheep in the nearby fields every now and again, but not that often that it would cause him concern. His strategies had been well thought out. Every miniscule detail intricately picked over until it fitted perfectly into place.

Ensuring the farmer wasn't out seeing to his sheep for some strange reason in the pitch-black, he made the move to take his captive inside the cottage. She was still out cold and, despite her being slim, he had to heave her limp frame out of the car and into the cottage. He had her room prepared. It was in the cellar. He'd built a couple of rooms, in fact, anticipating that he was going to be busy with an influx of guests over the coming week or so. He grinned and placed her on the thin mattress, against the stone wall. To the left was fresh running water, trickling down the walls. He'd get around to fixing that one day.

He locked the door and peered through the opening. She stirred, unsure of her surroundings. Her gaze travelled the length and breadth of the confined space. The fear crashed over her features like a large white wave in a raging storm.

Her focus landed on him watching her through the bars of the opening.

"Rest now. You're going to need all your energy for what I have in store for you."

"What? Who are you? Where do I know... you from? Stop, don't go... come back and answer me."

Her pleas proved pointless. He had no intention of debating the ins and outs of why he had abducted her or what his intentions were for her imminent future. "Make yourself comfortable, you're going to be here a while. There, in the corner, is a bucket. You're intelligent enough to figure out what it's for without me having to spell it out for you."

"Why? I need to know why you're doing this."

"All will become clear, eventually. Settle down for the night."

She sobbed. "But I don't want to be here. Can't we talk? Come to some arrangement? My husband will be expecting me. He'll get onto the police right away. They'll be out there searching for me. You're only going to get into trouble if you refuse to let me go."

"All valid points; I fear all nonsensical assumptions on your part, dear lady. Now, shut the fuck up and give that tongue of yours a rest." He walked away from the door and out of the cellar, banging the door at the top of the stairs behind him.

I'm going to enjoy getting rid of her when the time comes.

CHAPTER 1

A *week later.*

Sam walked along the road with Sonny and Benji behaving on their leads. Rhys had insisted he should come with her, to ease the pressure of handling both dogs, but he needn't have worried, she had them under control. Suddenly a Border collie came tearing at them off-lead. Sonny had been the first to react, tugging on his lead, eager to get to the dog to have an investigative sniff. "Sonny, be good. Don't do that."

The frantic owner of the collie came out of a nearby gate and grabbed her dog by the collar. "I'm so sorry, he's a nightmare when another dog comes close. He wouldn't hurt a fly, but his enthusiasm can get him into trouble at times. Are you all right?"

"I'm fine. I'm not used to handling two of them on a walk. No harm done. I'll be more cautious next time I come this way."

"It's the postie's fault, he left the bloody gate open for Rufus to escape."

"He seems a sweet dog."

The young woman got down and ruffled her dog's head. "He's not bad, mostly. A bit skittish at times, like most collies. However, I wouldn't be without him."

"They're family, drive us potty sometimes, but their love for us more than makes up for it, doesn't it?"

"It does. I must get a wriggle on or I'll be late for work."

"Me, too. It was nice meeting you. Take care." Sam continued on her journey to the park at the end of the road and let both the dogs off. She smiled, watching them chase each other, darting in and out of the trees and making their way over towards the bridge. She strolled down there, elated to see them getting on so well together. Mind you, they always had, since the first day they'd met, at this very park. It was the first time she'd laid eyes on Rhys, the new love of her life, who had recently moved in with her after Chris, her ex, or rather her soon-to-be ex, had walked out on her, leaving her with a mountain of debts to her name.

Thankfully, Rhys had persuaded her to let him take over half the household bills, including the large mortgage she and Chris had taken on in order for Sam to achieve owning her dream home. Maybe that had initiated the decline in her marriage, the day they'd moved into the cottage and started the numerous renovations needed to bring it up to modern-day standards.

Benji barked off to her right. He was standing next to a woman holding a yapping Jack Russell in her arms.

"Can't you keep your mongrel under control?"

"I beg your pardon, he's a pedigree Labrador, if you don't mind." The woman's attitude ticked her off more than it should have.

"Either way, it shouldn't be off the lead if you can't control it."

"Benji, here boy." Benji came right away and sat while she attached the lead to his collar. "See, he's obedient."

"Shame you were off with the fairies, daydreaming and not paying proper attention to your dog. You need to keep an eye on your dogs in this park. Is that one yours as well?" She pointed at a clump of trees where Sonny was bounding in and out of the river running just beyond them.

"Yes. He's having fun. Where's your sense of adventure? Dogs are allowed to roam freely in this park, in case you aren't aware."

"Well-behaved ones, maybe. Yours aren't. Now if you'll excuse me, I'm going to take Precious to the vet's to pick up her medication. I might get him to check her over while I'm there as well, after the shock she's just received."

"You do that. I'm sure you're making a mountain out of a molehill for no just reason."

"If you say so."

The woman stomped off, still mollycoddling her pooch in her arms.

Sam sighed. "Come on, Benji, let's gather your brother and get home. Want some breakfast, do you?"

Benji cocked his head at her and barked. Sonny came running to see what all the fuss was about, and she slipped the lead on his collar before he could set off on yet another adventure.

Sam enjoyed the stress-free, leisurely stroll back to the house. She waved at her lovely neighbour, Doreen, and raised three fingers, letting Doreen know how many minutes she expected it would take before she landed on her doorstep with Sonny. Benji would go off to work with Rhys, the way he always did.

"Hey, I was just about to send out a search party for you. Everything all right?" Rhys looked as smart as he usually did, in his light-grey pin-striped suit and black polished brogues. But it was his piercing blue eyes that always did a magnificent job of melting her insides whenever she peered into them.

"What? Oh, yes. A slight run-in with a busybody who made a point of laying down the law that goes hand in hand with how a responsible dog owner should act in the dog park."

His nose wrinkled along with his fair brows. "Am I supposed to know what that means?"

She laughed. "Me wittering on as usual. Can't abide people with nothing better to do, verbally mouthing off down at the park. It doesn't wash with me and makes me rather angry."

"I had noticed. What happened?" He quickly peered down at his watch.

"Nothing. There's no point in us being late because of that old biddy. You get off. What time will you be home this evening?"

"I have a late appointment, so probably at around seven. What about you?"

"That's the sixty-four-million-pound question. I won't know until I see what lands on my desk today. I can give you a call at lunchtime, how's that?"

He took a step towards her and gathered her in his arms. Pulling away from their long kiss, he said, "I'll look forward to it. I have to fly now, unless you want me to do anything before I leave? The kitchen is all shipshape, and I made the bed and tidied the towels in the en suite."

"You're extraordinary. Thank you. I'm going to enjoy you living here."

"Not just for the fringe benefits then?"

Her cheeks warmed under his searing gaze. "Those as

well. Go, you've embarrassed me enough this morning as it is."

He pecked her on the nose then swooped down to collect his briefcase and summoned Benji to join him. "Love you, see you later. Have a good day. I hope it turns out to be a quiet one for you."

She clenched her fists and covered her eyes and, shaking her head, she groaned. "Oh no, that's fatal, you saying that. I'm bound to be under pressure now."

"Ouch, sorry. I'm getting there. There's such a lot to learn when living with a copper. I'm bound to slip up now and again."

"Don't worry, go, I'll see you later. I'll call you at lunchtime unless my day is full on."

He smiled and closed the door behind him. She moved over to the bay window and watched him settle Benji in the back of the car and wave before he got behind the wheel.

She was so lucky to be with him. He had come into her life a little over six months ago and turned her world upside down. She'd never believed in love at first sight relationships, and no one was more shocked than she was when it happened to her, hitting her like a hammer blow. His car drew away. Sam left her position and gathered Sonny's bits and bobs that he would need throughout the day and deposited him next door with Doreen.

"Good morning. How are you today, Doreen?"

Her neighbour smiled and ruffled Sonny's soft fur. "I'm feeling well today. I saw you come back from your walk earlier. How's it going, with two of them to deal with?"

"Mostly good. They haven't pulled me that much, not really."

"I'm not sure I could cope with the two of them together."

"We will never expect you to, I promise, Doreen. Are you sure you can cope with Sonny? Just tell me anytime you feel you can't, won't you? I can always ask Vernon to look after him for a day or two." Sam's other reliable dog-sitter was her brother-in-law, Vernon, who was a professional footballer with Carlisle United but had recently been off with an injury. The second Chris had walked out on her, Vernon had volunteered to share the load with Doreen. It had taken a huge weight off her shoulders to have such reliable and selfless people surrounding her. It meant she could get through her working week without any added stress to consider.

"I'm fine. I'd soon tell you if I thought I was out of my depth with him. He's no bother when he's here at all. He and Ginger always have a brief run around first thing, but they soon settle down together."

"Glad to hear it. The last thing I want to do is put upon you, you know that."

"I know, now shoo, shouldn't you be getting to work?"

"On my way now." She handed Doreen the bag of supplies and bent to kiss Sonny farewell. He scooted past Doreen and into her hallway. "Make yourself at home, mate."

"Oh, he definitely does that. Have a good day, Sam. Don't work too hard."

"I'll try not to. Ring me if there are any problems. Thank you again for looking after him."

"Get away with you. I should be thanking you, not the other way around. He's a great source of comfort to me during the day." She smiled again and got ready to close the door.

Sam retreated and left her neighbour to get reacquainted with Sonny. She went back to the house and cast a quick eye around the downstairs. Everything appeared to be in its place, so she closed the front door and jumped into the car and headed into Workington.

She hadn't got far before she noticed something odd happening in her rear-view mirror. There was a van overtaking a few of the other cars behind her. Focusing on the van, in between keeping an eye on the traffic ahead of her, it didn't take her long to figure out who was driving it and what they likely wanted.

Bugger, it's Chris. How dare he hassle me like this on the way into work... any time actually? He needs to bloody get on with his life and leave me alone.

Once he was tucked behind her, he blasted his horn and flashed his lights. There was a lay-by up ahead. Sam indicated, pulled in and waited for him to get out of his vehicle. Not long after, he tapped on the window. She lowered it about an inch, enough to speak to him but not low enough for him to put his hand or arm through the gap.

Without smiling, she asked, "What's this all about, Chris?"

"I wanted to see you. Lower the window, Sam."

"Why should I? I've told you before, anything you have to say can be relayed to me via both solicitors."

"That's costing us both an arm and a leg and you know it."

"You had a choice. We didn't have to go down the route of having solicitors fight our battles, you started it."

"I wanted what was rightfully mine... half the house."

"You're insane. I don't even own half the sodding house, it mostly belongs to the mortgage company. Somehow you seem to have forgotten that important detail. Then of course, there was the issue about the loans you took out in my name. Who the fuck do you think is going to pay for them?"

He crossed his arms and slumped against the side of the car. "Why do you keep throwing that one at me all the time?"

"I wouldn't need to if you hadn't conveniently forgotten to tell your solicitor the truth about the debts. This is all your fault, Chris, no one else's. We were getting along just fine until you walked out on me... for three weeks, I might add, to move in with that tart of yours."

"You know that ended a long time ago."

"Not my problem you suddenly found yourself classed as homeless. You know what they say, the grass isn't always greener on the other side. I guess you found that out the hard way, didn't you?"

"Why do you persist in going over old ground? Can't we move on?"

She tapped a finger on the steering wheel in time to the beat coming from the radio. "Newsflash… I have. Whilst I'm sad things didn't turn out the way you had anticipated with your strumpet, my life has gone from strength to strength, and I have a wonderful man…"

"Back in your bed, that was what you were about to say, wasn't it?"

"I was going to add, in my life, but yes, he shares my bed with me."

"The bed we selected together when we furnished our first home," he seethed.

"Get over it, Chris. Hounding me like this is never going to achieve anything. Quite the opposite, in fact. It's going to put more of a wedge between us, if you must know. Now, was there anything else? I have to get to work. You know how much I detest being late for my shift."

"Another issue that killed our marriage… you working all the hours down at the station, not giving a shit about me at home, renovating the damn house that you were so desperate to get your hands on."

Sam ran her tongue around her teeth and checked her nails. "Same old mantra. Time to move on."

"I can't."

"That's *not,* I repeat, *not,* my problem. None of this is my problem."

"It snowballed out of control before I realised what I was doing."

She snorted. "I've heard it all now. From what I can

remember you were cheating with *her* behind my back for months, and when you walked out and became a permanent fixture in her house, well, that's when she must have realised her mistake."

He kicked out at a stone. "It wasn't like that."

"Bollocks, it was exactly like that. Do you mind? I have to get to work now. I'm sure you have a job you need to go to as well."

"I don't. The work has dried up now that things are getting back to normal after the pandemic."

"And you're expecting me to feel sorry for you, is that it?"

"Showing some compassion has never been a problem for you in the past."

"Perhaps, for the right people. Not my ex."

"Technically, I'm still your husband."

"No, technically, you're my cheating bastard of a husband."

He launched away from the car and stared at her. She could see the cogs turning and his expression changed several times until he finally found his voice. "Give me one more..."

She gasped and shook her head. "No way. I can't believe you would have the audacity to stand there and ask me to take you back. You're sick, not in your right mind if you ever thought that was on the cards. My advice to you is to leave Workington. It will be better for both of us if you did."

"Sod off! Why should I be the one to leave?"

"You just told me you have no work here, so leave, find work in a different, more suitable area, and allow me to get on with my life."

"I am allowing you to get on with your life."

"You are? If that's the case, then why are you standing here, pleading for me to take you back?"

"I wasn't, not in so many words. Sam, I love you. I've never stopped loving you."

"Even when you had your cock up someone else? How can you stand there and talk such drivel?"

"It's true. She meant nothing to me. It was you who I came home to every night."

"Except for the three weeks in which you just took off. You didn't even bother to contact me to tell me that you were okay. And after all that, here you are, pleading with me to take you back. Get a life, Chris. I have one, and it no longer includes you in any aspect of it. See you around." Sam started the engine and quickly left the lay-by to filter into the traffic once more. She glanced in her rear-view to see Chris staring after her, a livid expression twisting his features out of place. She didn't care. He'd started all of this, and thankfully, she'd had the sense to end it. Not many women would have been able to, she was aware of that. She was happy, deliriously so with Rhys by her side. He had never let her down from the moment he'd swept into her life, and she had a feeling he never would in the future, either.

On the drive to the station, she couldn't help speculating if she'd been a tad harsh on Chris. She wasn't usually the confrontational type, he'd forced her hand there. Made it impossible for her, and the only way she could get out of the situation was by lashing out verbally at him. Now she was wondering if she'd overstepped the mark. Flung one too many insults at him. *What's done is done, there's no taking back the words now, Sam.* It had never been in her nature to be vindictive, those who knew her well would agree with her perception.

The station came into view. She inhaled and exhaled a few calming breaths to help lighten her mood. Sam parked in her allocated space and studied herself in the mirror for a second or two. *You've got this... this morning was just a blip. He'll be out of your life soon enough, once the divorce is finalised. Not long to wait now.*

Walking through the main entrance, she paused to have a quick chat with Nick, the desk sergeant. "Hey, how are things at home with your wife?"

"Ah, morning, ma'am, thanks for asking. She seems a lot better now the HRT has started to kick in. Life is far more bearable for all of us. Less shouting for no reason. I don't have to walk around on eggshells whenever I'm at home."

"Ah, a blessing in disguise, that one then. Glad the doctor was willing and able to treat her symptoms properly. There is talk that a lot of doctors tend to dish out antidepressants like Smarties to a lot of women, instead of accepting the inevitable and putting them on HRT."

Nick shook his head. "Shame on them. The difference is far more noticeable than either of us bargained for."

"Glad to hear it, Nick. You're an amazing husband for putting your wife and her needs before your own."

He smirked. "Blimey, I wouldn't put it quite like that myself, ma'am. I love her and was willing to do what it took to get her back. Hormones have a lot to answer for, ruling a woman's body the way they do. I admit it, you women have a lot to contend with throughout your lives. Let's just say, I'm grateful I was born with meat and two veg."

Sam covered her flaming cheeks with her hands and laughed. "Oh my Lord, I think that's got to be the line of the week, right there. You do come out with the strangest sayings, Nick."

"Sorry, I suppose I forgot who I was talking to for a moment or two then."

"On that note, I'd better begin my day in earnest."

"I think we both had. Sorry if I caused you any embarrassment."

"You didn't, you lightened my mood, which I'm grateful for."

She punched her passcode into the security keypad, entered the inner sanctum and climbed the concrete stairs to the incident room. Bob was the first to turn her way. He smiled, leapt out of his chair and headed for the drinks area to fetch her a coffee.

"Morning all. Everyone doing okay?"

Her partner joined her. He had two cups of coffee in his hands. "All fine and dandy with me. What about you?" His eyes narrowed.

She averted her gaze from his, fearing he might be able to read what was going on in her mind. "All okay with me. Thanks for the caffeine fix. I'll be in my office, dealing with the morning dross. You have my permission to interrupt me if anything vying for my attention crops up."

"Will do. Until then, I've told the rest of the team to finish up the paperwork on the cases we've recently wrapped up."

"Good thinking. I'll be with you in a few hours." She took her drink into the office, removed her coat and sat behind her desk to survey the paperwork that was crying out for her attention. She took several sips of coffee and opened the first letter. After reading the contents, she tucked it in her in-tray to deal with later. She took another few sips of coffee then booted up her computer to check her emails. There were at least ten requiring her immediate attention.

Bugger, why do they do that? Hit us first thing. Why can't headquarters send the emails during the day, so we can tackle them as and when? Why put bloody pressure on us at the start of our day, for Christ's sake?

She tried to rid herself of the negativity that had already seeped into her working day and got down to the business of tackling her post and emails. She hadn't been at it long when there was a knock on the door and Bob poked his head into the room.

"Busy?"

She wafted her hands over the paperwork. "Take a guess. What's up?"

"Umm… a dead body has just been found. I think it has our names written all over it."

"What? Seriously?"

He rolled his eyes. "No, not literally. Sorry for misleading you. I think we should take a look, that's what I was trying to say."

Sam leapt out of her chair and slipped on her coat before she followed him out of the office. "You can fill me in on the way."

They reached the main entrance. "My car or yours?" Bob asked. He'd not long had his cast removed from his injured leg and was keen to keep using it, so they had agreed to use his car for the last week or so.

"I'm easy either way."

"Mine it is then." He pressed the key fob, and the doors opened.

"Where are we en route to?" Sam strapped herself in and asked.

"Derwentwater. A female's body was found out on the lake. She's been shot."

Sam's head whipped around to look at him. "What?"

"You heard me, she's been shot. Don't ask me anything else, that's all I got from the control centre."

"I take it the pathologist is already at the scene?"

"Yep."

"Did he request that we join him?"

Bob groaned. "I don't think so. It was pot luck we got the case. That's not good, is it?"

"It's okay. I'll still be having a word with Des. I'd rather he informed us directly in cases of this magnitude. Shot… unbelievable in this neck of the woods. Not sure we've… nope, I'm not going there, just ignore me." Sam cringed, suddenly remembering the mass shooting that had taken place in the area back in 2010 by Derrick Bird. The incident had consisted of a major manhunt. The killer had travelled the west of Cumbria, indiscriminately killing his victims. There had been over thirty crime scenes to attend during the incident. At the end of his vile mission, he'd turned his gun on himself, denying the families of the deceased from having their day in court. In the community's eyes, he had literally got away with murder.

Every time the case reared its head, it caused every officer on the force to speculate if they had done enough that day to prevent the slaughter of so many innocent lives.

The rest of the journey was conducted in silence.

"Are you all right?" Sam asked.

Bob applied the handbrake and faced her. "It'll never leave us, that damn case, will it? Every copper I know can still remember what they were doing on that day and how inept they felt."

"I know. It's better if we don't dwell on the whys and wherefores of it. Mistakes happened. Thankfully, nothing as bad as that has ever happened in this area since. We've played our part in ensuring that's the case, Bob."

"I agree. But then, here we are, attending yet another murder scene. When will people in this bloody community begin to live with one another?"

"Stop it! It's not just our community going through these horrific times. Incidents as grave as the one we're about to attend are happening throughout the world at any given moment. You only have to watch the news bulletins every night to realise that, Bob."

"Granted, although it doesn't make it right, does it?"

She unhitched her seatbelt and opened the car door. "Nope, it doesn't. Chin up, let's see what Des can tell us about the case."

Bob lashed out at the steering wheel, venting his anger on the inanimate object, and followed her across the road to the awaiting SOCO vehicles.

"Come no closer, not until you get togged up," Des raised a hand and bellowed.

"We've run out. Sorry, that's not an excuse. We came in Bob's car and forgot to pick up supplies in our eagerness to get here."

"Amateurs," Des grumbled. "You'll find what you need in the back of my van. Don't take extra supplies and leave me short because you screwed up. We're on a tight budget as well as you guys."

Sam tutted at her partner and took a step back. "We'll be with you in a tick."

"In your own time. The victim isn't going anywhere, not anytime soon. We've already erected a marquee over her. Looks like the rain will be with us soon enough."

Sam didn't respond. She and Bob searched for, and removed, a couple of paper suits from the rear of Des's van, and Sam watched the pathologist make his way back to the edge of the water. Not long after, his assistant joined them.

"Hey, Vanessa, how's it going?" Sam asked.

Judging by her expression, the young assistant appeared to be down in the dumps. "It's okay, I suppose. He's keeping me busy today."

"Ah, giving you the runaround, is he?"

"You could say that. Keeping me on my toes would be more accurate."

"Poor you. You need to stand up for yourself more if he becomes too much."

"No chance of that happening. I enjoy my job, I'm here to serve him."

"Okay, but you need to stand your ground at times. I've heard the way he speaks to you, it's not pleasant, and you shouldn't have to put up with that crap." Bob nudged her in the ribs. "What? It's the truth. You come to work to assist your colleagues, not to expect them to bully you."

Bob sighed. "It's not our battle, boss."

"I know. I just hate the thought of women being taken for granted by their male associates."

Vanessa smiled. "I don't think that's the case, Inspector. I truly believe he speaks to everyone the same."

"I'm glad to hear it, but he still needs to be brought to task over his attitude now and again. Look at you, I can tell you're on the verge of tears. That can't be right, love, can it?"

"Keep out of it," Bob advised through clenched teeth.

Vanessa walked back towards the crime scene, and as she passed Sam, she whispered, "Thank you for caring. It's not all that bad. I have a few personal issues I'm having to deal with at present, as well."

"Ah, you should have said. I feel foolish now for putting my foot in it."

Vanessa smiled. "Sorry. It'll sort itself out soon enough."

Sam glanced at her partner who was shaking his head.

"See, I knew there had to be more to it," he said.

She pulled a face at him and trudged after Vanessa who took them to assess the body of the victim, but first they had to follow procedures and sign the Crime Scene Log. That particular task completed, Des welcomed them, if somewhat grudgingly, into the fold.

"Ah, there you are. All kitted up, I see. Well, here she is. A female who I'm guessing has an approximate age of around thirty. It's possible that age might be extended a couple of years on either side. Blonde, slim build, no obvious signs of injuries, apart from the gunshot wound to her head."

"How long has she been in the water?" Sam queried.

"A rough guesstimate at this stage would have me believe that she entered the water last night."

"And who found the body?" Sam cast a glance over her shoulder in both directions and spotted a woman in her mid-to-late fifties talking to a uniformed female officer alongside a patrol car.

"The witness speaking to one of your lot. She had been for a quick dip in the lake, saw something in the distance and swam out to investigate. Poor woman nearly drowned when she saw the state the body was in. She called out for help, and a couple of fishermen came to her rescue. They're down there. Gone back to their pitch to try and catch tonight's dinner, no doubt."

"Great. At least they're all still here. We'll have a chat with them. What else can you tell us about the victim? Any ID found on her? I'm surmising that's wishful thinking on my part, yes?"

"You can't have it handed to you on a plate all of the time, Detective Inspector Cobbs, you should know that by now."

"Anything else? Any idea what type of weapon was used?"

"Stating the obvious, a gun. I'm not an expert in the field, however, I know a man who is. I'll be calling on him for his professional opinion. I'm not one to speculate, as you know."

"When is that likely to be?"

"I'll make the call as and when I have the time," Des replied sharply.

"Or you could give me the name of your contact and I could put the request in, if you're as snowed under as you say you are," Sam countered. She struck the air with an imaginary finger. *Take that, you obnoxious pig.*

Des was okay in the main, but every now and again he

showed signs of chauvinistic traits that in the good old days he would have probably got away with. Not these days, and definitely not when dealing with Sam. Given the opportunity, she would slap him down the second she suspected him straying off the well-trodden path and into the rough.

"You're right, now why hadn't I thought of that? Remind me to give you his details before you leave."

Sam nudged Bob. "Or we could get that out of the way right here and now, just in case it slips either of our minds later."

A smirk tugged at the corners of Des's mouth. "Smart lady."

"In my defence, you don't get to become a DI if you're a thick bitch."

"Touché."

Des gave Bob his associate's details, which her partner jotted in his notebook.

"You say the woman found the body way out in the lake. How did it get out there, any idea?"

Des stared at her for a second and asked, "What am I, psychic? I'll do my best to piece things together but because water is involved, some puzzle pieces are going to be impossible to find with this one."

Sam scanned the area. There were trees to the sides of them. "Could the killer have been hiding amongst the trees and taking a pot shot at her?"

"It's possible. I fear SOCO are going to have a tough time with this location, it's vast. Yes, the victim was pulled ashore at this point, but look how immense this damn body of water is. Who knows where she entered the lake? How she got out in the middle, fully clothed, I might add?"

Sam scratched the side of her face as she thought. "When you put it like that, the only logical explanation is that someone took her out there via a boat of some kind."

"A fair assumption. Now all we have to figure out is where and when she was shot. Was it before or after she was dumped out in the lake?"

"Which is why we need the expert's advice to guide us," Sam suggested.

"It will probably benefit us, yes, agreed."

"Okay, I can tell you have a lot of work ahead of you, so we'll leave you to it unless you have anything else for us?"

"Not at the moment. You'll be the first to hear when I do."

"Thanks, Des. We'll have a chat with the witnesses."

Des nodded abruptly and then crouched by one of his technicians alongside the corpse.

Sam and Bob made their way over to the woman who had found the body. They stripped off their paper suits en route and deposited them into the awaiting black bag.

"Seems strange that a killer would go to the trouble of being seen, taking the victim out into the middle of the lake by boat, don't you think?" Bob asked.

"Nothing about this case so far is adding up, I believe we're going to be dealing with a mountain of speculation in order to find the truth."

"One thought, if I may?"

Sam paused mid-stride and faced her partner. "Go on. I'm all ears."

"Before we speak to the weapons expert, isn't he bound to want to know what kind of bullet or cartridge has been used?"

"Fair point. We'll sound him out first, and then I'll chase Des up for the information."

"If you want my opinion, I think we should leave Des to get in touch with his friend. Maybe he gave us his details… umm… setting us up to fail from the outset."

Sam glanced back in the pathologist's direction and studied him through narrowed eyes. "Would he do that?"

"Tick him off often enough, he's bound to seek revenge, like any other bastard out there."

"Did I? Tick him off?"

"I'm not saying you did, but sometimes I get the impression..."

"What? You can't stop there!"

Bob walked on ahead and mumbled, "I get the impression that he digs his heels in."

She trotted after her partner and yanked on his arm, forcing him to face her again. "Are you winding me up? Telling me that you believe sometimes he puts obstacles in our way during an investigation?"

"I know I talk a lot of bullshit at times, just forget I said anything."

"Great, thanks for putting bloody doubts in my mind before the investigation has even begun to take shape."

"You're welcome. It's up to you if you take what I say on board or if you cast it aside."

"I always listen to the advice you have to offer, so don't toss that one in my direction." She continued along the path that led to the witness, her mind already working itself up into a tornado of possible scenarios to do with the case.

"Sorry, I didn't mean it to come out like that, boss."

"Apology accepted. Can we just start the day over and see where it leads us, eh?"

"Sure thing. Sorry."

"And stop apologising, it's pissing me off." She turned his way and grinned.

He mouthed the word 'sorry', and she swiped his arm. "Okay, professional heads back on. Let's see what the witnesses can tell us."

The woman had damp hair and was dressed in a pale-pink tracksuit with go-faster white stripes down each of the legs and arms.

Sam gave a brief nod to the female constable standing nearby and showed her ID to the witness. "DI Sam Cobbs and DS Bob Jones. I understand you're the lady who found the body, is that right? Sorry, I haven't been told your name."

"It's Carol Morton. That's right, I come swimming out here most days and have never, ever in all my days, had to deal with anything as tragic as this."

"I'm sorry about that. What time did you arrive here?"

"After first light, at around eight."

"How soon after did you discover the body?"

"By the time I got changed and had a splash around in the water, I suppose I spotted the woman around ten to fifteen minutes later. I couldn't work out what it was. Curiosity got the better of me. I wish to God it hadn't. The shock at finding her sent me in a tizzy. How I got out of that water alive… Christ, it's unthinkable what might have happened if I hadn't found it in me to cry out like that. The two men who rescued me, they deserve a ruddy medal. Between them, they managed to pull me and the body back to shore." Tears bulged and dripped onto her pale cheeks.

"Are you all right? I know that probably sounds like a daft question at a time like this. What I'm saying is, do you think you should get checked over at the hospital?"

"I think I'll drive over there and see what they have to say. With the shock I took in a lot of water. I dread to think of the number of bugs et cetera I might have swallowed."

"I agree. I believe there would be no harm getting examined by a doctor. I can arrange for you to be taken there, if you'd like. I wouldn't feel right about you driving all the way to Whitehaven by yourself."

"I would feel such a fraud. I'm perfectly all right, it's the victim you should be concerned about, not me."

"No, that's not right at all. If someone has experienced any form of shock, it should never be ignored."

"Thank you for your sympathy. In that case, I'd like to take you up on your offer."

Sam looked at the female constable. "Can you give Carol a lift to the hospital?"

"Of course, ma'am."

"Good, that's settled. Before you go, would it be okay if I asked you a few more brief questions?"

Carol smiled. "Yes, that's fine."

"When you arrived or during the time you've spent here, have you seen anyone else in the area?"

"Apart from the two fishermen who assisted me, no, I don't believe so. Mind you, I can't say I've been on the lookout for anyone either."

"What about when you arrived? Did you see any other vehicles lingering in the area?"

"Let me think. Yes, there was a black car driving away from the parking area where I always leave my car."

Sam's interest piqued. "Did you notice who was driving? The make and model of the car?"

"No, sorry. I wish I could tell you more. It was a fleeting glance, nothing more."

"Don't feel bad. You've given us something to go on at least, for which I'm grateful. You get yourself off to hospital. I'm going to give you my card. If anything else regarding the vehicle or the driver should come to mind, please let me know."

Carol took the card and nodded. "I will. You think someone killed her? There was a wound on her head. One of the fishermen thought it looked like a bullet wound. I wouldn't know, but I find it hard to believe anything as sinister as that could go on in these beautiful surroundings."

"It did appear to be. We've yet to carry out a post-mortem on the victim. That will give us a better insight into what we're dealing with. I appreciate you hanging around to speak with us. Please take care of yourself. Thank you for going above and beyond for the victim."

"I don't think we had a lot of choice. We decided between us that it would be the right thing to do, bringing her in, rather than leaving her out there to be feasted on by the fish and birds visiting the lake."

"Nevertheless, it took courage and guts all the same."

"We had a moral obligation to do what was right for her. I don't regret my actions. She's back on dry land now, we couldn't leave her out there."

"It was admirable of you all. I hope you get a clean bill of health from the hospital."

"Thank you."

Sam took a step back and nodded for the constable to leave the area with the witness.

"That took some guts, from all of them," Bob said.

"You could say that. Let's see what the fishermen have to say."

They made their way over to where the men were set up, outnumbered by their rods.

"Hi, gents," Sam said. "Apologies for disturbing you. Have you managed to catch anything today?"

"Only a dead body, that about sums up our day," the older man responded.

"James is right, I think we should pack up and go home. The fish have obviously been scared off by all the activity going on in the water already this morning."

Sam smiled. "Only natural, I suppose. Do you come down here regularly, James and...?"

"He's Will. Yep, at least once during the week and on a Sunday, weather permitting, of course," James said.

"There are times when we'll chance our arms and come out when it's raining as well," Will chipped in.

"Do the fish bite better or worse in the wet?" Bob asked.

"About the same," Will replied.

"I didn't know you were interested in fishing, Bob," Sam said.

"I've had my moments over the years. It can be frustrating sitting on a soggy bank for hours on end without so much as a bite. Ain't that right, chaps?"

"Too right. We mostly come down here for the peace and quiet, to get away from all the crowds, and sometimes our nagging wives, but don't drop us in it with our better halves."

Sam smiled. "Your secret is safe with me, don't worry. Do you always pitch in the same spot or do you vary your positions?"

"We tend to favour this spot more but we do venture over to the other side of the lake in the summer when there are more people visiting the area. The enjoyment isn't the same when you have screaming kids running in and out of the water in the height of the season, and the fish definitely bite more when the water is undisturbed. Good days are few and far between when there's a lot of noise down here. People can be so inconsiderate to others these days." James sighed.

"I can imagine. Going back to what happened earlier today, I take it you were already set up and fishing, yes?"

"That's right. We got here at around eight or thereabouts," James said.

"I have to ask if you saw anyone else out here around then," Sam queried.

"Nope. We tend to concentrate on what we're doing, setting up the tackle and sorting out the bait."

"You know the victim was shot. What about the noise of a gun? Anything sounding like one being shot around that time?"

"No, can't say there was. Do you know how long the body had been in the water? Can you even tell that?" Will asked.

"A rough guesstimate is that she had been in the water since last night."

James shrugged. "Would the killer hang around after he got rid of the body?"

"That's what we're trying to establish. There's no set way these types of people conduct themselves. He might well have dumped her and hung around to ensure he'd killed her, perhaps fallen asleep in his car and left this morning at first light."

"Hard to believe someone would risk being spotted like that," James said.

Sam bit down heavily on her tongue, she had said enough already. "Indeed. We're going to need to take a statement from you both within the next few days, if that's okay, gents?"

"Yep, we'll do whatever you need."

"If you give my partner your full names and addresses, we'll pass your details to the desk sergeant who will slot you in. A uniformed officer will make arrangements to come and visit you sometime today. Thanks for doing what you did earlier and coming to Carol's assistance."

"Our pleasure. No one likes to see a damsel in distress, do they? Sorry we couldn't help the victim sooner," James said with a shudder.

"You did your best, that's all anyone can ask. Thank you again." Sam stepped away, leaving Bob to gather the information needed to go forward. She stood at the top of the bank and surveyed the area around the lake, wishing she had a set of binoculars to view the far side of the expanse of water. It was a perplexing investigation from the outset, one that she wasn't relishing sinking her teeth into, not with so many variables already on the table.

Who is she? What has she done to deserve to be killed? Why shoot her and then dump her body here? Or was she dumped and then the killer toyed with her, left her stranded and took pot shots at her from the bank? If that was the case, where did that all take place? Why?

"Did you hear me?" Bob raised his voice beside her.

"Jesus, man, you scared the shit out of me. You could see I was deep in thought."

"I know. Care to share what's going through that head of yours?"

"Lots, too much to mention. We're knee-deep in possible scenarios on this one already."

Bob glanced over his shoulder at the lake beyond. "You're not kidding. Who the bloody hell dumps a body out here, at a beauty spot such as this?"

"A fucker with a warped mind is the best I can come up with at this stage."

"Yep, that one would definitely get my vote. Where do we go from here?"

"We're going to need to rely on the relatives of the woman coming forward to report her missing."

"Would it be worth scouring the whole area? See if there's a vehicle parked up somewhere that might be abandoned?"

"You could be on to something. Call the station and get that organised, will you, Bob? No, on second thoughts, I'll do it on the way back to the station, while you drive. Let's see if Des can add anything else first, before we leave the area."

"You're brave, going near him a second time, the mood he's in."

Sam sniggered. "Yep, you've got to feel sorry for Vanessa, putting up with daily shit from him."

"You worry too much. I reckon she's tougher than she looks."

They walked back to the car. Des was getting something out of the back of his van.

"Anything else of note we should be concerned about, Des?" Sam sidled up beside him.

"Nothing yet. How did you get on with the witnesses?"

"They couldn't really add anything, except the woman, who thought she saw a black vehicle leave the area as she arrived this morning."

His nose twitched as he mulled over the news. "Hmm… unlikely to be the killer's vehicle if she was dumped in the water last night. That is, if my preliminary assessment is correct."

"I thought that, but then, it also occurred to me that maybe the killer hung around all night, possibly fell asleep after his exertions of getting her out there in the middle of the lake."

"It's possible. We'll do a search of the area where the witness was parked, just in case."

"Makes sense. I take it you're aware of where that was."

"I am. I'll organise a search now."

"Talking of which, we're going to see if we can flood the area with a search team, see if they can find anything to help with the investigation."

Des raised an eyebrow and inclined his head. "On one proviso."

Sam's stomach rolled over. "What's that?"

"They keep out of our way. Sometimes uniformed officers need to use a little more restraint, in my experience."

"I'll be sure to pass on your concerns to the desk sergeant."

"Good. I must get back to it."

"Yep, ditto. Will you get the PM results back to me soon?"

"The same time frame as usual."

Sam and Bob climbed back in the car and left the area. Sam made the first of her calls. It was to Nick, the desk sergeant. She relayed her request to have feet on the ground, searching the area, and added Des's concerns not to interfere with the zone they were working in. Nick agreed to action her request immediately and to get back to her personally if they found anything of value during the search.

The second call was to the weapons expert. As suspected, he told her he couldn't really give much advice without seeing the pellets or bullets that were used to kill the victim. She told him that Des would be in touch with him once the PM had been performed later that day. She hung up, feeling dejected.

"Hey, don't you dare feel bad about this," Bob reprimanded her.

"Ha, you know me so well. I fear this one is going to test us all the way."

"How can you think that when the investigation has only just commenced?"

"Defeatist attitudes never help, do they?"

"Too right. We'll get there, we always do, boss."

CHAPTER 2

Sam searched the Missing Persons' files that had been registered online in the past month or so. She was shocked to see so many within a fifty-mile radius.

They pulled three interesting names and printed off the photos. Sam compared them to the photos she had taken of the victim at the lakeside that morning and decided the third woman was a close enough match.

"What do you think?" She went back into the incident room and handed the photo to Bob.

He turned it to the left and to the right and held it close. "Is that a mole on her face? I noticed the victim had one this morning."

"I had forgotten all about that. Yes, I think you're right. The hair colour is similar. Granted, the victim's hair was wet, so that would alter the look of it slightly."

"She appears to be the same build. Hard to tell what colour eyes she had, but the lips and nose seem very similar, if not the same," Bob admitted.

"Yep, all points I thought of myself. Glad we're on the same page. Looks like we've got a name for the victim: Fern

Mitchell. We've got contact details for her husband. Let's get on the road again, Bob. I'll drive this time."

"I don't mind, it's your choice."

They left the station and drove thirty minutes out to the address they had on file for the husband. There was a silver Mercedes sitting in the drive of the detached house on a relatively new estate.

"How long has this place been here, any idea?"

Bob shrugged. "Pass, not an area I come to that often. They seem fairly new, maybe a year or two at the most. Why?"

Sam smiled. "Being inquisitive, that's all."

"Your mind is going to get you into bother one of these days."

They left the car and walked up to the house via the narrow path, separating two small lawned areas and a few shrubs that the developer had obviously put in before handing over the keys to the new owners. Sam rang the bell and waited for the door to open. It took a few moments until a man in his late twenties to early thirties opened it.

"Yes?"

Sam showed her warrant card and introduced them. "Mr Mitchell, is it possible to come in and speak with you?"

"I take it this is about my wife. Have you found her?"

"It would be better inside, sir," Sam insisted.

He gave a brief nod and allowed them to enter. Sam and Bob followed him through the clean and tidy short hallway into a square lounge dominated by the biggest television that was apparently all the rage these days. A sofa was positioned on either side of the screen, and there was a large glass table in the space between them. He gestured for Bob and Sam to take a seat.

His brown eyes appeared sunken and had dark circles

around them. "Please, what do you know? Have you found her? Is she alive? Has she lost her memory?"

Sam and Bob sat on the sofa opposite the one he'd sunk into. She held up a hand to suppress any further questions. "I'll answer your primary question first."

He sat forward, on the edge of the grey fabric, and placed his forearms on his thighs, then linked his hands together. "I'm waiting."

"This morning we discovered the body of a woman who resembles your wife."

His gaze shot between Sam and Bob and returned to Sam. "What does that even mean?"

"A body was rescued from Derwentwater this morning, and we have reason to believe it could be your wife."

"I… umm… what? Either it is or it isn't. Which is it?"

"We've made a comparison to the photo you supplied to the Missing Persons Team, and there is a distinct likeness. However, because the body was found in the water and the pathologist believes it has been there overnight, her features are slightly distorted."

"Slightly distorted? Do you have a photo of her? You must have. Any copper worth their salt wouldn't come away from the scene without taking a photo, would they?"

"I have. Please, I'd rather not distress you by showing you the photo right now."

"Why? What's the next step in the process? I know what it is, you don't have to spell it out for me. So what's the difference in me seeing a photo of her now and me coming down to the mortuary in the next day or two to go through an identification process?"

"You seem pretty clued up on these things. May I ask what you do for a living, sir?"

"It's Wayne, and I'm a teacher, a biology teacher, so you could say I'm an expert on how the body works. For instance, I'm assuming her body hasn't been affected that much, given how cold Derwentwater is. Of course, it would depend on what depth she was found, that makes a difference to the decomposition of a person's body, as does the length of time she has been in the water. If you say it appeared overnight, then I'm safely assuming that she's not that bad."

The man's blasé attitude flummoxed Sam for a few seconds. She glanced at her partner for assistance. Bob let her down, keeping his gaze trained on the victim's husband.

She cleared her throat. "I wouldn't do this ordinarily, but I believe you've put your point across too well to ignore your request." She removed her mobile from her pocket and scrolled to her latest photo. She angled the phone in his direction. He took it and gasped.

"That's her. There's no doubt in my mind." He continued to stare at the photo for a long time and even traced her face with a finger. "Wait..." He glanced up at Sam. "Is that a bullet wound? Was she shot?"

"Another reason why I hesitated in showing you the photo. Yes."

"How? Why? She was such a good swimmer, too. When you said she was found in the lake, I thought at least she died doing something she loved." He studied the picture again and whispered, "Is she fully clothed? She is, that's what she was wearing the day she went missing. I'm so confused."

Sam ran her tongue over her dry lips. "So are we. When we returned to the station and searched through the Missing Persons' files, we noticed that it has been almost a week since you reported her missing."

"That's right. She failed to come home after she went to the pub with a few of her colleagues on Wednesday of last week. I rang the station and was told that I couldn't report her missing for a full twenty-four hours, so, am I over-thinking this? My wife went missing last week, and her body was discovered after being dumped in the lake last night, so where has she been all this time?"

Sam shrugged. "That's what we're desperately trying to find out. My guess would be that she was more than likely held somewhere for a week before she was killed."

Wayne Mitchell swiped a hand over his pale cheeks. "My God, this doesn't seem feasible to me. None of it is making any sense. Why shoot her? Aren't guns illegal in this country?"

"Mostly, yes. But there are some people who are allowed to have them under the proviso that they're stored in a locked cabinet."

"What are you saying? That they're okay to use them as long as they're returned to a cabinet?"

"Unfortunately, yes."

"This gets worse. Do you know what type of gun was used?"

"Not yet. That will be revealed after a post-mortem has been carried out within the next forty-eight hours."

He fell back in his seat and placed his hands on top of his head. "I can't believe this, any of it. Why do this to her?"

"Maybe you can give us a little insight into your wife's character, her likes and dislikes and whether anything has happened in her life lately that would cause any concerns?"

"She was a hard-working teacher who enjoyed nothing more than sitting with her class, encouraging them to do well at school. She took her role in their lives very seriously. Determined they would move on from primary school with their heads full of knowledge that she had added there, in her own inimitable way. She made learning fun for the kids, always came up with lessons designed to include every pupil. She was proud of their abilities to be pushed when she felt it was needed. There were no slackers in her class, everyone was a willing participant every day they attended her classroom."

"She was well loved by the pupils, that's lovely to hear. What about the other members of staff, how did she get on with them?"

He frowned and raised his chin to stretch out his neck. The bones clicked a few times during the process. "Everyone loved her at the school. They were amazed by the way she treated and taught the kids."

"Amazed? Did her willingness to go the extra mile for her pupils ever cause friction between her and the rest of the staff?"

"No, never. I can't believe you would ask such a question."

"Sorry, it's my job to delve deeply into a victim's relationships."

His eyes narrowed. "Ah, I wondered when this conversation would come back to me. That is what you're about to ask next, isn't it, Inspector? Whether we had a rocky relationship or not."

"Sorry, yes, it's procedure, not meant to cause offence, sir."

"On the whole we were good. Every marriage goes through its rough patches, I defy anyone to tell you otherwise."

Sam and Bob glanced at each other, knowing how true that statement was regarding their own relationships in the last couple of years. "I agree."

"But I would never, I repeat, never, harm a hair on that woman's head. I loved her. I may not have liked her at times, but that didn't mean I had ever fallen out of love with her."

"How long were you married?"

"Our fifth wedding anniversary would have been in December." He closed his eyes and shook his head.

"I'm sorry. Forgive me for the probing questions."

"I understand. Although it doesn't make it right. I wish you'd take my word for it. I wasn't involved in her murder. I was deeply in love with Fern."

"Can you give us the names of the people she was out with last Wednesday?"

"Yes, hang on, let me get my phone, I have all their contact details in there." He eased himself off the sofa and left the room. He returned within seconds with his iPhone in his hand. After punching in his passcode, he scrolled through the screen with his finger. "Here we are, the first is Justine Wordsley. Do you want to jot the details down?"

Bob held out his hand for the phone, and Wayne gave it to him. Bob wrote down the contact details for the first friend and handed the phone back to Wayne.

"The second one is Lisa Jolly." Again, he gave the phone to Bob to note down the relevant information. "And the third one is Mandy Davidson."

Bob took the phone a final time and returned it to Wayne who went back to the sofa and put the mobile on the cushion next to him.

"Have you heard from any of them since?" Sam asked.

"Oh yes, we've been in constant contact. We've been going out there regularly to search for her, as a group. Lisa printed up flyers, and we've posted those around the town. I genuinely believed they would help, but nothing could be further from the truth. We haven't received a single call, not even a prank one, which I'm led to believe by the experts is to be expected in cases like this. Where could she have been until now? Someone must have abducted her, that's my belief. Although when she first disappeared, it did cross my mind that she might have run off with someone else."

Sam's interest rose. "You had concerns about that?"

"It's bound to surface if your wife goes missing and there's no sign of her for a week."

"Did she have a vehicle with her at the time she went missing?"

He nodded. "Yes, that was found abandoned in a farmer's field on Saturday."

"Ah, this is the first I'm hearing about it. Where?"

"A few miles out of town."

"We'll investigate it, see if SOCO have had a chance to examine the vehicle. I presume they still have it?"

"Yes, it was damaged anyway."

"Damaged? In what way?"

"The front wing looked as though it had a prang with something. The copper who came to see me to report the car had been found thought that she had possibly hit a hedge."

"Are they sure another vehicle wasn't involved?"

"I don't know. You'll have to make enquiries into that yourself."

Sam smiled. "We'll do it as soon as we get back to the station. My assumption after hearing that would be that she either had an accident or possibly that she might have been forced off the road with the intention of kidnapping her."

"I never even thought about that. Why? Why kidnap her? Look around you, we don't have money coming out of our ears. We're both teachers, and this place is mortgaged up to the hilt. It took us years to come up with the funds to put a ten percent deposit down, the rest belongs to the mortgage company, well, it would do if we defaulted. Not sure how I'm going to cope paying all the bills on my own now, what with the energy bills on the up and up. Good job I'm out at work all day, that's all I can say."

"The prospect of your wife having been kidnapped, once again leads me to ask if she's ever fallen out with anyone."

"Not that I can remember."

"What about past boyfriends? Did she have anyone hanging around of that ilk?"

His mouth pulled down at the side as he contemplated the question. "No, we've been together off and on since we were at university. I think she went on a few dates in between, but they were one-offs, never anything more than that."

"I see. And you always got back together within a few months of parting?" Sam asked.

"Not really, more like weeks."

"Okay. And you haven't noticed anyone hanging around the house when you've come home from work?"

"Nothing out of the ordinary. I've not noticed any strangers on the estate at all, not lately."

"Can you tell us what pub she went to that night?"

"Yes, the Lord's Tavern, do you know it?"

Sam clocked Bob nodding out of her peripheral vision. "My partner does, that's good enough for me. Do you know at what time she left that night?"

"The others said it was around seven-thirty."

"And she told them she was coming straight home or did she say she was stopping off somewhere en route?"

"No, straight home. My wife enjoyed her food, she rarely skipped a meal. She was intending to cook my favourite meal that night."

"And where were you?"

"I was in a meeting with one of the students and his parents at the school. We had several issues to sort out. The usual, stopping bullying as soon as we are made aware of it."

"And what school would that be?"

"Westlands."

"And the meeting went well?" Sam asked.

"Yes. The boy was shell-shocked to have been discussing it in front of his parents. I doubt if he'll get up to any mischief in the future."

"Glad to hear it, that'll be less hassle for us further down the line. And your wife, where did she teach?"

"At Acorn Croft."

"Thank you. You told us that you and your wife's three friends all went out searching for her. How often?"

"As often as we could, given that we all work full-time as teachers. None of us could afford to take time off, so we met up every other night, other commitments permitting."

"And they all went willingly?"

"Yes, every single one of them. They all wanted her back as much as I did. They're going to be devastated to hear the news. I suppose that's going to be down to me to tell them, isn't it?"

"If you'd rather we did it, I don't mind."

"I would be grateful. I'm only just holding it together as it is. If I saw them break down in tears, I'm sure it wouldn't be long before I crumpled into a heap myself."

"Don't worry. We can do it, more than happy to, in the circumstances. Is there anything else you think we should know?"

He shook his head slowly. "I can't think of anything."

"Did Fern have any other relatives living in the area?"

"Yes, she was local. Lived here all her life. I can give you her parents' address and phone number, if that'll help?"

"It will, thanks."

He searched for the information and again gave it to Bob to jot down.

"What happens now?" Wayne asked.

"The post-mortem will be performed, and the pathologist will be in touch with you soon after to let you know when you can visit your wife's body."

He shuddered. "That's going to be awful, and yet I wouldn't want it any other way. I need to say farewell to her in person. I'm glad her body has been found so that I can move on. You hear of so many stories where the families fail to get closure when a loved one goes missing."

"I understand completely. We'll pass on your details to the pathologist. He'll be in touch to make the necessary arrangements with you."

"Will that be all? I need time alone now, to process the news."

Bob slapped his notebook shut beside her, and they both got to their feet. Wayne showed them to the front door, and Sam shook his hand.

She then gave him one of her cards. "Sorry the news couldn't be better. Sincere condolences for your loss."

"Thank you. Just promise me you'll get the person responsible for killing her, make them pay for ruining our lives together. We had our future all mapped out. Fern had a scrapbook of all the places around the world she intended to visit. Now I have nothing to look forward to, without her."

Sam rubbed his arm. "I'm sorry, that's one of the hardest things, losing someone and the dreams that were never fulfilled."

He gave a weak smile and opened the front door. "Will you keep in contact with me throughout the investigation?"

"We will, as soon as we have any news worth sharing. Bear with us, though, I fear it's going to be a frustrating case initially, but you have my word that we'll do our very best to achieve an arrest swiftly."

"Thank you. I hope that proves to be the case."

Sam waved, and she and Bob walked back to the car. "My leg is a bit sore."

"Don't worry, I'll drive." She slipped into the driver's seat. Wayne had left the front doorstep and moved to the bay window in the lounge to watch them drive away.

"What did you make of him?" Bob asked, fastening his seatbelt.

"If you're asking me if he is behind her abduction and murder, I'd have to be honest and tell you that I'm not sure."

"He seemed upset enough, although he didn't break down, as such. I thought that was a little odd."

Sam waved her hand from side to side and then started the engine. She drew away from the kerb and said, "We both know that some men struggle to express their feelings openly."

"Yeah, I'm one of them, sort of."

"You think so? I wouldn't say that at all. There are times where I see evidence of you wearing your heart on your sleeve."

"Ha, not that often, I hope. And don't let the missus hear you say that. In her eyes I'm an uncaring bastard who lacks feelings most of the time."

"Forgive me if I don't believe you." She turned to look at him.

He grinned. "All right, maybe I went a tad OTT there."

"Typical man. And you're always proclaiming that women are the ones who tend to exaggerate."

"I am not. Anyway, getting back to the job in hand, where are we going now?"

"I thought we'd drop by and have a word with the women Fern was out with the night she went missing."

He sucked in a sharp breath.

"Come on, let's have it," she said.

Bob exhaled the breath. "I think it's too risky, showing up at the school during the day and breaking that sort of news to them."

Sam mulled over his reservations and sighed. "All right, why don't we scrap that for now and pay the pub a visit instead?"

"Agreed. You could always ring the school, speak to the Head and make arrangements to drop by at lunchtime. That way, when you break the news, they'll have time to recover before they get back to work and face the kids."

"Hark at you. 'Time to recover' after me revealing that one of their best friends has just been found murdered?"

"Now you're just being pedantic."

"Don't sulk. Look up the number for Acorn Croft and I'll speak to the head now."

"In other words, you don't trust me to do it."

"Did I say that? Okay, you win. You do it, that way I can concentrate on the road instead."

He grumbled something indecipherable and placed the phone on speaker during his call.

"Hello, Acorn Croft, how may I help you?"

"Yes, this is DS Bob Jones of the Cumbria Constabulary. Would it be possible to speak with the headmaster or headmistress today?"

"Let me see if she has any appointments free this afternoon," the secretary said, her tone bright.

"Sorry, it would be better to see her around lunchtime, if possible?"

"Oh, I'm not sure about that. Mrs O'Connell prefers to keep her lunchtimes free to deal with any teachers' queries that crop up during the day."

Bob faced Sam. She turned to him and made a pushing motion with her hand.

"It is concerning one of your teachers. Please, this is an important issue that needs to be dealt with quickly. Can you oblige?"

Sam sniggered at his choice of words, and he dug her in the ribs.

"Hold the line, I'll check with Mrs O'Connell." Orchestral music filtered down the line.

"Stop taking the piss or I'll leave you to do all the work

next time. This is supposed to be lending a helping hand, in case you've forgotten."

"I haven't. Wind your bloody neck in, man. What's wrong with you? You can't seem to take a joke these days. Testy as a cat with a flea infestation most of the time."

"I am not."

The music stopped playing. "Hello, sorry to keep you waiting. Okay, Mrs O'Connell has agreed to see you at twelve-thirty, if that's acceptable to you."

"We'll be there. Thanks very much. Shall we report to reception upon our arrival?"

"Yes, we have split shifts to cover the lunch hour. I'll be on duty to greet you."

"Thanks, look forward to meeting you in person."

"Me, too."

Bob ended the call, and Sam chuckled.

"Look forward to meeting you in person," she repeated, taking the mick.

"Jesus. Are you going to have a pop at everything that comes out of my mouth today?"

"Not necessarily, depends if it's worth it or not. Lighten up, Bob."

"I was making a serious call, and here you are, taking the frigging piss out of everything I say."

"Hardly. I apologise, profusely. I shouldn't have done it."

Bob crossed his arms in a huff and hunkered down in his seat. Sam turned on the stereo, and he groaned.

"What's wrong now?"

"Bloody Smooth Radio, repeat, repeat, repeat. There are millions of songs out there, and I bet, over the course of the week, they play about five hundred of them, over and over again."

"Stop moaning. The music is mellow, just what we could do with on a ride out to the pub."

"What I could do with is downing a few pints when we reach the other end. I have a feeling that ain't gonna happen, is it?"

"You know the answer, so why even bring it up?"

"Worth a try. Going for the sympathy vote."

"Sympathy vote?"

"Yeah, you having a pop at me unnecessarily and me mistakenly believing that you'd want to address any upset caused."

Sam laughed, she couldn't help it. "Dream on, pal. Dream on."

"You might want to take the next left up ahead. I think the pub is halfway up the road on the right, from what I can remember."

"Thanks, nice to know you can still talk sense some of the time."

He turned to look out of the side window and cursed under his breath. Sam suppressed another laugh and pulled up outside the main entrance in the large car park. "Come on, sulker, let's get in there."

"Or I could leave it to you and stay in the car and grab forty winks."

She called his bluff, opened the car door and got out without saying another word. He shot out of the car and caught up with her on the circular steps of the old pub. Sam liked the look of this place. The exterior was mainly built of red brick, and there were dozens of hanging baskets strategically placed around the façade, all planted up with winter flowers, such as pansies. It gave the pub a nice, homely feel, and the inviting atmosphere continued when they entered the public bar. A large inglenook fireplace with an open fire roaring, took the chill off the enormous beam-filled bar.

"This place is stunning. I can't believe I've never visited it before," Sam whispered.

"I've been a few times. The food is quite good, the Sunday lunch is top notch."

"Shame we have a lunchtime appointment elsewhere, we could have strung out our visit and I might have treated you to a sandwich and pint."

He raised an eyebrow. "Drinking on the job? You'd never catch me risking my pension, boss."

"Yeah, me neither. Bad call on my part. I'm going to see if I can twist Rhys's arm to bring me here at the weekend."

"Sounds like a plan. There's the landlord."

Sam produced her warrant card, and they both walked towards the bar.

"Hi, are you the landlord?" Sam asked.

"I am. Dave Irton. Who wants to know?"

She flashed her ID, and he leaned forward to study it. "Police, should I be concerned?"

"I don't think so. We're admiring your pub. Have you been here long?"

"About fifteen years, give or take a few months. That's why you're here, to admire the facilities?"

Sam smiled at the confusion etched into every crevice on his tanned face. "No. We're here about something that may have happened last Wednesday."

"Either it did or it didn't, which is it?"

"I'm not really making myself clear, am I? Let me start again. We're investigating the murder of a young lady who we know came to your establishment last Wednesday evening."

"A murder? Of a regular, you say?"

Sam raised a finger. "That I'm not so sure about. Apparently, she came with three other friends after they'd finished work for the day."

"As do a lot of people. As far as I'm aware, not many of them get murdered. Did this person have a name?"

"Fern Mitchell, do you recognise it?"

He paused, and his chin lifted in the air. "Can't say I do. Do you have a photo?"

"Yeah, I'm not sure you'll be wanting to see that."

"Dead in it, is she?"

Sam chewed on her bottom lip for a second. "Yep."

He grimaced and frantically shook his head. "Yeah, you did a wise thing, not showing me. How can I help?"

"We wondered if you might have any CCTV footage from that night."

"Think she met her murderer in my pub, is that what you're telling me?"

"Nothing of the sort. However, at this early stage, it's the only lead we have to go on, because her husband reported her missing not long after she left the pub."

He frowned. "Forgive me if I'm wrong, but I thought you had to wait twenty-four hours before reporting someone missing."

"You're absolutely right. Let me correct myself. The husband realised she was missing later that evening. He rang the station but was told to file a missing person report the following evening, after the twenty-four hours were up."

"Poor bloke. Fancy going frantic about her whereabouts only to be stifled by the coppers. What did he do? Give up?"

"He had a sleepless night, I should imagine. Anyway, Mr Irton, would it be possible for us to view the footage?"

"It's Dave. Why not? I usually keep all the discs for about a month before recording over them. Want to come through to the back?" He gestured for them to circle the bar to the opening on the other side.

"Great, we appreciate your assistance."

He showed them into a larger-than-average office-cum-storeroom that was tidier than most she'd been in the past few years. In their line of work, calling on the local hostelries to obtain vital camera footage which often resulted in the arrest of criminals earlier than the other long-winded routes they sometimes had to take to conclude an investigation.

"Take a seat, there are a couple of spare ones in the corner."

"We're all right, we'd rather stand to get a better view."

He flicked through several CD cases and held one up in his right hand. "This will be the one you're after, then. Any idea what time I'm looking for?"

"Around seven-thirty her husband seemed to think."

"Let me see what I can find for you then." He inserted the disc into the machine and trawled through it to seven in the evening.

Sam noticed a group of women seated on one side of the room and pointed. "Could that be them?"

Bob took a step closer to the screen. "Not a hundred percent sure, but I think it might be."

"Ah, yes, I remember the ladies," the landlord commented.

"As in they were boisterous or causing trouble?" Sam asked.

"Oh no, nothing bad. A few raucous laughs, you know what women are like when they get together."

Sam glanced his way and raised an eyebrow. "No, not really."

"Oops, I guess I've put my foot in it again." His awkwardness came with flushed cheeks.

"It's okay, I was only joking. Can we move the disc on a little?"

Dave did as requested. They watched Fern leave the bar area alone, around twenty minutes later.

"Why do women do that?" Bob asked.

"Do what?"

"Leave the damn pub on their own."

Sam shrugged. "Maybe because they have respect for

humanity and don't believe anything is likely to happen to them. We're entitled to walk around by ourselves, just like men are."

Bob raised his hands. "I wasn't suggesting otherwise."

"Good. Dave, what about cameras showing the car park, are we in luck there, as well?"

"I'm sure we can sort you out. I can ditch this one then, nothing much to see here, right?"

"Keep it to one side for now, we might need to revisit it again later, it depends on what we see next."

Dave stopped the recording and switched the discs to the cameras focused on the pub's exterior.

"I'll whizz along to the time the woman leaves the pub. We can always come back to moments before if it's needed," Dave suggested.

"Go for it. Stop! That's her leaving now." Sam's gaze fixed on the grainy image. "Why are the cameras outside the pub always so much worse than the ones inside? Sorry, that's not having a dig at you, Dave, we see it time and time again."

"Maybe the weather conditions have an impact on the cameras, who knows? Shall I move it along now?"

"Yes, sorry." Sam kept with the victim, and her pulse rate shot up when a man approached Fern and appeared to hold a conversation with her, if only a brief one. "Interesting. Let's keep going forward and return to that section in a while."

They watched the conversation between them end not long after. Fern went to her car, and they saw her leave the car park, followed by a black Ford Puma, the number plate of which had been removed, or so it would seem at a quick glance.

"I'm not liking the look of that guy," Bob announced.

"I have to agree," Sam said, blowing out an exasperated breath. "What we're going to need is a copy of this section.

From what I can tell, he's tried to avoid the cameras where possible, except when he spoke to her."

"Why would he do that? The temptation getting the better of him or what?" Bob asked.

"Your guess is as good as mine. Judging by the fact his number plate has been removed, it's likely that his intentions were premeditated."

"What are you saying, that this man came to my pub in the hope he would pick someone up, or are you telling me that he had the woman earmarked as a target already?" Dave shook his head, clearly finding either concept hard to believe.

"We don't know the ins and outs of everything yet. We'll need to get the disc analysed by experts first, before we get carried away and make assumptions along those lines."

"I'll sort you out a copy now. I'm shocked by what I've seen."

"In fairness, all we saw was a man talking to the victim and leaving the car park immediately after her. That really isn't much to go on," Sam summed up.

"It's enough in my book," Bob replied.

Dave hit a couple of buttons and, within a few minutes, he removed a disc from the machine and slipped it into a plastic case. "There you go. Can I help you with anything else?"

"Maybe supply us with a copy of the footage showing the group while they were sitting in the bar area?" Sam asked.

"Of course." He inserted the previous disc once more and made a copy of that one as well, and then handed a second plastic case to Sam, once the recording had been finished.

"We can't thank you enough for your help, Dave," Sam said, grateful for his assistance.

"Always a pleasure to aid the police when possible. I hope

it helps. Do you think he's the one who killed her? Or is that a daft question?"

"It's looking more and more likely to me. We're so thankful your cameras were able to pick up his image."

"Sorry it's not clearer, but at least you've got his car caught on camera, as well. That's got to help, hasn't it?"

Sam crossed her fingers on both hands and raised them in front of her. "One can only hope, even though his plate was missing. Thanks again for your help."

They retraced their steps through the hallway to the bar. Sam smiled at Dave.

"If you need extra copies or want to ask any further questions, I'm on call most of the day, seven days a week," he said.

"What, no day off during the week?"

"Nope, not since the pandemic, can't afford to have that luxury."

"I understand. The hospitality industry took, and is still taking, a huge hit."

"You're not kidding."

"I hope things turn around for you soon, Dave."

"Thanks. Good luck with your investigation. Will you use the footage at a press conference?" he asked, his eyes sparkling.

Sam winked at him. "We might do, you never know."

"Mind you, thinking about it, if you mention the pub as where the victim was approached by the killer, maybe it's going to do this place more harm than good."

Sam winced. "Yeah, perhaps you're right. I'll see if I can work around that when the time comes to hold a conference."

She and Bob left the pub. Outside, Sam scanned the area. "He came from that direction so would have had a perfect view of the victim exiting the pub. Did he make his move then? Or are we barking up the wrong tree? Could he be an innocent bystander in all of this?"

"I'd probably go along the lines of the latter, except… you seem to be forgetting his number plate was missing. That reeks of intent."

She nodded. "Okay, let's get back to the station and go over the footage with the others."

CHAPTER 3

The incident room was buzzing when they arrived. Claire requested Sam's attention as soon as she entered the room.

"What's up, Claire?"

"I received a call about five minutes ago, boss, from the victim's mother. She sounded upset. I told her that I'd ask you to call her back as soon as you returned."

"With respect, she's bound to be upset after hearing the news, isn't she?"

"I got a feeling there was more to it than that. I might be talking out of my arse, though."

"Leave it with me, I'll give her a call. Do you have her number?"

Claire slipped her a sheet of paper with the number written on it.

"Anything else happen while we've been gone?"

"No, not really."

"Okay. Bob, can you set the discs up? Show everyone what we have and then get to work trying to trace that car through other cameras and ANPR in the area, please."

"Leave it with me."

Sam headed into her office and removed her coat which she hung on the stand next to the window. She noted the time on her watch. It was already eleven-fifteen, and they had an appointment to keep at the school at twelve-thirty.

After sucking in and releasing a few deep breaths in preparation, she sat and dialled the number, which was instantly answered by a breathless woman.

"Hello, is that Mrs Thomas?"

"It is. Is that DI Cobbs?"

"Yes, it's Sam, Mrs Thomas. First of all, I'd like to offer my condolences for your loss."

"Thank you. Fern was our world, she was our only child," she said before breaking down.

"I'm so sorry."

She sniffled and whispered, "Thank you."

After a moment's awkward silence, Sam asked, "You called the station a little while ago, wanting to speak with me?"

"I did. I wanted to get in touch, firstly to ask you to do all you can to uncover the truth and..."

"And?" Sam prompted gently.

"And to tell you what I know."

Sam stared hard at a mark on the wall, and it morphed into Fern Mitchell's face. She shook her head to clear the image from her mind. "Which is?"

"That all was not as it appeared to have been at home."

The words came like a sucker punch to Sam. "Sorry, would you care to elucidate for me?"

"No doubt Wayne gave you a cock-and-bull story about how happy they were together, didn't he?"

"In all honesty, he told me they had their ups and downs like any other couple. Are you telling me it was far worse than that?"

"She was about to leave him. At least, that's what she implied the last time we spoke."

"And when was this?"

"The Saturday before she went missing. We had lunch in town together and, to be honest, I've never heard her speak so openly about her marriage."

"You haven't? Do you mind sharing with me what she told you?"

Mrs Thomas paused for a while and then sighed. "She told me she felt her marriage was over."

"Ah, that's interesting. Was he aware of her intention to leave?"

"I'm not sure."

"Had Fern mentioned to Wayne that she wasn't happy?"

"Yes, I believe, several times."

"Were they working through their differences?" Sam asked.

"I think it was too late for that."

Sam shuffled uncomfortably in her chair and picked up her pen. "Are you telling me someone else was involved?"

Silence.

"Mrs Thomas, are you aware how your daughter died?" she asked tentatively.

"Yes, he told us. I find it incredible to believe that someone would shoot my daughter. I need to know how and why this happened, DI Cobbs."

"I assure you, my team and I are giving it our all to find out."

"I'm glad to hear it. I hate to say this, but I think you need to dig into Wayne's alibi a little deeper."

"Are you saying what I think you're saying? That you believe your son-in-law might be behind your daughter's death?"

"I'm planting the seed, Inspector. I don't have any proof

as such, only what my daughter told me about the state their marriage was in the week before she went missing. I'm not really one for believing in coincidences but, to me, it's what I think you'd call a no-brainer, is that the correct term?"

"It is. I'm sorry, but I'm going to have to have far more than hearsay to go on. Was your daughter seeing someone else?" she asked a second time, aware that the question had been brushed past already.

"Yes. Another woman."

"Oh, I see. Were they seeing each other? Intimately, I mean?"

"Yes, they were lovers and intending to spend the rest of their lives together."

Sam scribbled down some notes on a clean sheet of paper. "Does this woman have a name?"

"Ivy, I believe. That's all I know. Don't you think it's strange that she should share this information with me one day, and a few days later she goes missing, then turns up… well, dead? I find it incredible to imagine, but those are the facts."

"It's leading to a possible motive, if that's what you're asking. However, I'm going to need evidence to back up your claim."

"My claim, as you put it, is a fact. My daughter revealed the truth about the state her marriage was in, all I'm doing is passing on that information to the officer in charge of the case. If you have no intention of delving into the truth, then maybe I should speak to your senior officer, see if they're interested in what I have to say."

"There's no need for you to do that, Mrs Thomas. I'm listening to what you're telling me, but as I've already stated, I can't accuse Wayne of any wrongdoing with no evidence or proof to guide me."

"What else do you need then?" Mrs Thomas asked sharply.

"To speak with Ivy, that would be a good place to start. Do you have her contact details for me?"

"I don't. Nor do I have her surname."

Sam shrugged as if the woman was in the room with her. "Then there really is little I can do at present."

"What? You're prepared to brush this information aside? May I ask why?"

"I'm not trying to be awkward with you, Mrs Thomas, but I'm going to need more. Like, who this woman is, where they met. Anything that we can research further."

"Oh, gosh, I can't give you any of that information. It's taken a lot out of me, as you can imagine, trying to process all of this after hearing earlier that you had found Fern's... body. I've lost my daughter. All I'm trying to do is be helpful, and here you are, putting a block on that."

"I'm not, not really. I have to be practical and work within the law, Mrs Thomas. Families fall out all the time. For all I know, you might have some sort of grievance against Wayne."

"Well, I've heard it all now. What the hell! What type of person do you think I am?"

"Someone who is grieving, rightly so. Just to clarify, I'm not for one instant saying that I don't believe you. All I'm doing is trying to obtain further information."

"I'm fully aware of what you're trying to do. I can't furnish you with anything other than what I've told you already. I read about it all the time in the newspapers, a husband or wife scorned, and they seek their revenge. I'm not saying Wayne killed my daughter, but he might have paid someone else to do it."

"In my experience, that only tends to happen in the movies."

Mrs Thomas growled. "I can see we're not getting anywhere fast here. I'm going to see what my husband says about this later and then take the matter further. Give me the name of your senior officer."

"Certainly, it's Detective Chief Inspector Alan Armstrong. I'm sorry you feel this way. I'm sure when you speak with him, he'll back me up. We have certain procedures in place that we are forced to adhere to. Without further details, I won't be able to pursue the matter. I hope you understand my dilemma."

"Not really. Goodbye, Inspector."

The line went dead. Sam threw her pen across the room. "Shit! What the fuck am I supposed to do now?"

Bob appeared in the doorway. "I heard a clatter. Is everything all right?"

"Not having the best of days, partner. How are you getting on?"

"I've contacted a couple of the shops close to the pub. They've both got cameras and are sourcing the footage for me. I told them we'd pick it up later."

"Good idea, we could either pick it up on the way back from the school or send one of the guys out to do it instead. No, on second thoughts, we'll do it en route. If we nip out now, we should have enough time to collect the discs before our appointment, then we can come straight back here and get down to business with the information we gather from her friends."

"You mean, *if* we gather anything valuable from her friends," Bob grumbled.

"I'm trying to think positively, despite getting kicked around the room by her mother."

"Ouch, you'll have to fill me in on the way."

"Are you ready to go?"

"All good for me."

. . .

Of the two shops they called upon, one had the relevant disc ready for collection but the other didn't, forcing them to hang around for fifteen minutes while a member of staff hurriedly muddled her way through making a copy on the antiquated machine in the back office. By the time the job was finished, Sam got the impression the woman had exhausted herself mentally and physically for the day. She mumbled an apology and handed the disc case to Sam.

"There's no need to apologise, we're grateful for your assistance in this urgent matter. Thanks again for going to all this trouble for us."

"It's okay. I hope it helps your case."

Sam smiled and left the shop with Bob. Racing to the car, she was aware how late they were, and she took the decision to use the siren to get them through the heaving traffic until they were within a few streets of the school. They entered the main entrance with two minutes to spare. Sam's insides churning up a storm, they approached the receptionist to announce their arrival.

"Ah, yes, we've been expecting you. I'll let Mrs O'Connell know that you're here, if you want to take a seat."

Sam smiled. "We're fine."

The receptionist darted down the hallway and returned a few minutes later. "If you'd like to come this way, Mrs O'Connell will see you now."

They followed her into the headmistress's office, and Mrs O'Connell welcomed them with a concerned smile.

Sam and Bob produced their warrant cards.

"DI Sam Cobbs, and my partner, DS Bob Jones. We appreciate you agreeing to see us at such short notice, Mrs O'Connell."

"I'm intrigued to know what all this is about, Inspector."

Straightening her back to sit upright on the edge of her chair, Sam delivered the heartbreaking news. "It is with regret I have to inform you that a few hours ago we discovered the body of Fern Mitchell."

Mrs O'Connell covered her gaping mouth with her hand and shook her head. She swivelled in her chair to face the window behind her and blew her nose on a tissue.

"Are you all right?" Sam asked.

Eventually, Mrs O'Connell spun around to face them, her eyes watering. She dabbed at them with a fresh tissue. "I'm sorry for breaking down, it's been a horrendous week for all of us, not knowing whether something serious had happened to her or if she had simply taken off somewhere to get some peace and quiet. We've all done our bit, been out there with Wayne, every time we had a spare moment."

"I can tell she was well liked. I'm sorry the news has come as a shock to you."

"I have to ask, where was she found?"

"In Derwentwater. I'm afraid there's more. She was shot. We're not sure if that happened before or after she entered the water."

"My God! Why? Who would do such a thing to our Fern? You're aware that she was an excellent swimmer, I take it?"

"Yes, her husband told us as much when we broke the news to him earlier."

"Damn. How did Wayne take the news? Sorry, ignore me, that's such a silly question."

"I wouldn't say it was silly, it was an obvious question. He seemed to be genuinely upset."

Mrs O'Connell wiped her eyes again. "The teachers are going to be distraught. Fern was very popular with the other members of staff and also with the children... Oh my, I can't quite believe this is happening. Murdered, I can't get my head around this. If you had come here and told me that she'd died in an accident, then fair enough, however, learning that her life has been robbed by foul means is, well, it's near impossible to understand."

"I know. Losing someone so close to us by such an awful crime is never easy."

"The others need to know. What a dilemma I find myself in now. Should I break the news to them now or after school? Either way, they're going to be traumatised. If I delay telling them, they might never forgive me."

"My advice would be to get it out of the way as soon as possible, to avoid such repercussions."

Mrs O'Connell jumped out of her chair and tore towards the door. "Yes, I agree. I think we'd better do it this instant. We can chat afterwards, if you need to."

"Whatever is best for you."

Sam and Bob left the office and walked alongside Mrs O'Connell, down the corridor to a room near the bottom, the staffroom.

The woman in her late forties paused at the doorway and drew in a few breaths. She glanced at Sam and asked, "How do you do it? Deal with death every day? This news has rocked my world."

Sam shrugged. "I can assure you, it isn't easy, but the need to find the killer in cases such as this drives us on."

Mrs O'Connell closed her eyes for a moment and then, once she appeared to be more composed, she entered the room with Sam and Bob a few steps behind her. "Sorry to interrupt your lunchtime, everyone, but I have some important news to share with you all." She hesitated to peer over her shoulder at Sam and Bob.

Sam gave her a tight smile and a brief nod.

Mrs O'Connell's chest rose and fell swiftly. She faced her colleagues again and moved over to a small bookcase at the side of the room. She leaned against it to announce the news.

"I'm sure you're wondering who these two people are. Well, they're police officers."

A sea of worried faces turned Sam's way and then returned to Mrs O'Connell once more.

She cleared her throat and said, "They've come to share some sad news with me today. I have to tell you, it's grave news indeed, that I never thought I would hear in my lifetime."

"Is this about Fern, Mrs O'Connell?" a blonde woman wearing a colourful dress asked.

"Sadly, yes. Unfortunately, Fern's body was found this morning. And the police are investigating it as foul play, a murder inquiry."

Everyone in the room looked as stunned and shocked as the headmistress had when Sam had broken the news to her. It took a few minutes for the news to sink in fully before people's emotions emerged.

One woman, a redhead who had a pair of spectacles slipped through her hair on top of her head, tore across the room to the sink in the corner. Another woman, sitting in the chair next to her, raced to be by her side.

"Are you all right, Lisa?" Mrs O'Connell asked.

There was no response as the woman continued to bring up the lunch she had just eaten.

Mrs O'Connell put the woman's distress aside for the time being and addressed the rest of the group. "I know how devastating this news is to everyone and I apologise for giving it to you at this time, however, we're going to need to deal with this, and as harsh as it may sound, get back to work soon. It's imperative we put on our bravest faces in front of the children, we've all had to deal with grief in the past. We're consummate professionals at the end of the day. Saying that, you know my door is always open if you need a shoulder to cry on or if you find you're struggling. Now the officers would like to have a word with you all."

Sam took a step forward. "Thank you, Mrs O'Connell. We're very sorry for your loss and understand and appreciate how devastating this news must be to you all. We are indeed conducting a murder inquiry and would be interested in speaking with three people in particular." Sam flipped open her notebook and read out the names of the three friends who had been with Fern the night she had gone missing.

Two of the women were over at the sink, one continuing to be sick and the other comforting her, while the other lady, who was sitting on the same table, raised her hand to let herself be known.

"We'll need a chat with all of you. Why don't we start with you?" Sam pointed to the woman at the table who nodded. "Would it be okay holding the interviews here, Mrs O'Connell?"

"Of course." She glanced at her watch. "You're aware that there is less than twenty minutes before the bell goes for the afternoon session?"

"It's cutting it a bit fine, but I'm sure we'll manage. We wouldn't normally do this, but if I can speak to the three ladies in question at the same time, my partner can interview the rest of you. We'll be as quick as we can but if we run out of time, we'll have to come back another day."

Mrs O'Connell wrung her hands. "Sounds like a good idea to me. If everyone is in agreement, let's do this as efficiently and effectively as possible. Lisa, are you well enough to speak with the inspector now?"

Lisa was facing them and wiping her mouth on a tissue. "I think so. I'm sorry for my reaction."

Sam smiled and gestured for her and the other lady to retake their seats. "Are you all right to interview the others, Bob? Just ask the basics: what she was like, if she had shared any grievances with any of them, if they had noticed anyone lingering around the school premises. Any fallings-out with parents."

"Blimey, all that within twenty minutes?"

Sam nudged him with her elbow. "Do your best."

Then she joined the three ladies who had taken their seats again around the table and asked the same questions. Sam found it difficult racing through the questions. To be honest, she found it gravely unfair on Fern's friends to bombard them with the same questions she'd instructed her partner to ask during their grieving. "I'm sorry to put the pressure on you ladies at this sad time, but if there is anything you can tell me that you believe may lead us to the person responsible for Fern's death, it'll be a massive help to our investigation. As it is, evidence is very thin on the ground at the moment."

"What type of thing do you want to know?" Lisa asked, her voice catching in her throat.

"For a start, you all knew Fern better than anyone else, I take it?"

They all nodded.

"Can you tell me if she had been concerned about anything lately?"

The three women glanced at each other. Sam tried to read the signals passing between them and took a punt on what each of them was thinking. "Wait, there is something that came to light this morning when I spoke to Fern's mother. She mentioned," Sam leaned over the table and lowered her voice to nothing more than a whisper, "that Fern was seeing someone else. All three of you knew her well enough, right? Was she?"

Lisa nodded. "Yes, a woman. She confided in us that she was about to leave Wayne. Oh God, don't tell me he had anything to do with her death, did he?"

"Don't think that, Lisa. He's been so upset from the

moment she went missing," Justine stated. "He's been out there with us, searching for her at all hours."

Lisa's eyes narrowed. "I'm aware of that. He could have been doing that to prevent suspicion landing on his shoulders."

Justine glanced down at her hands. "I don't believe that for one second. Fern informed me that they were having marriage difficulties but also said that she hadn't told him about the affair."

Sam jotted down the information, then asked, "I see. Okay, do any of you know who this woman is and where I'm likely to find her?"

"Yes, she's called Ivy Kitson and works at Wayne's school."

"What?" Sam asked, shocked. "Is she a teacher?"

"Yes, she teaches music over there," Justine replied.

"Did you all know about the affair?" Sam asked them.

The three women nodded.

"She swore us to secrecy," Mandy replied.

"How long had she been seeing this woman?"

Lisa wrinkled her nose. "Maybe three to four months."

"How did the affair start?" Sam asked.

"Fern went to see her husband one day and literally bumped into Ivy in the hallway," Lisa said. "She told us there was an instant attraction between them and one thing led to another."

"One thing led to another?" Sam asked for clarification.

"Ivy asked her out for a drink, and they hit it off right away."

"And all this was going on behind her husband's back? Are you sure he didn't have an inkling?"

Lisa shrugged. "Maybe he sussed it out and was pretending not to know, you know, acting as if everything was all hunky-dory between them."

"When it clearly wasn't." Sam's mind whirled up a storm.

Could Wayne be responsible for his wife's death? Did he find out about the affair? Why was their marriage in turmoil, if he didn't know about the affair...? Something doesn't add up to me.

"It's called life. None of us are truly able to control such powerful emotions when they strike," Justine added.

"Had Fern ever been interested in women before she met Ivy?"

"I don't think so," Lisa replied. "She never mentioned anything to me. What about you, Justine and Mandy?"

The two women stared at each other and shrugged.

Sam glanced at her watch. She had ten more minutes before she'd need to call the questioning a day. "What do you know about Ivy? Was she involved with someone else when the affair began?"

"No, not as far as I know," Lisa said.

"Did Fern tell you what their intentions were?"

Justine nodded. "Yes, they were going to tell Wayne and then set up home together."

"When were they going to do that?"

"Who knows? We all have a tendency to say things but never follow through with them in the end."

Lisa tutted. "That wasn't about to happen with Fern and Ivy. They fell for each other quickly and were determined to be together soon."

"Soon? Can you be more definitive for me?"

"Not really," Lisa replied, "we've told you everything we know about the situation. I'm sure Fern didn't tell us every little detail that went on in her life. We all prefer to keep some things back, don't we?"

"I suppose that's true," Sam was forced to admit. "Okay, ladies. Thank you for all the information you've shared with me today. I'm sure it's going to be a huge help towards our investigation."

"Glad we could help. She meant everything to us. The

world is going to be a much sadder place without her around," Lisa said.

She linked hands with the other two women who nodded in agreement.

Tears bulged in the women's eyes, and they hugged each other.

"I'll leave you to it. Thank you for speaking with me. I realise how hard this must have been for all of you. Once again, I'm sorry for your loss. Here's my card, if you need to get in touch."

"All we ask is that you do your utmost to bring this person to justice," Lisa said.

"You have my word that my team and I will do what it takes for that to happen." Sam pushed back her chair and walked over to have a word with Mrs O'Connell.

"How did it go?"

Sam smiled. "Well enough, in the circumstances. They're all very strong women. I was amazed by their resilience. They didn't falter once while I was asking my questions."

"Hopefully, their strong resolve will carry them through the rest of the day. What about your partner? Is he almost finished? We're running out of time now." She tapped her watch.

"I'll check in with him. We'll be out of your hair soon enough, I promise." Sam headed across the room to check how long Bob was likely to be.

She stood alongside him. He flipped his notebook shut and thanked the man and woman with whom he'd been speaking to. They rose from their seats and left the table.

"Anything of importance?" Sam asked.

"Not really. How about you?"

"We'll discuss it on the way back. Let's get out of here." She paused at the doorway and faced all the teachers. "I want to thank you all for taking the time to speak with us today, especially as your emotions must be running high right now."

Mrs O'Connell joined Sam at the door. "We wanted to do what was right for Fern. Hopefully we've all played our part in your investigation."

"We've gathered some vital information. We're grateful to you for allowing us to speak with your staff, Mrs O'Connell."

"Good, good. I'll show you out."

The three of them walked to the main entrance and Sam left a handful of business cards. The headmistress shook their hands and wished them good luck with the investigation.

Halfway back to the car, Bob said, "That was tough. The teachers I spoke to couldn't tell me much at all."

"I definitely had the better deal. We need to head over to the husband's school now."

"Eh? How come? Isn't he at home, or have you forgotten that?"

"Not at all. Now would be the perfect time, with him out of the way."

He faced her and frowned. "Is that one of those cryptic clues?"

"I'll tell you in the car."

Sam did just that once they were on the road.

"Bloody hell. Did Wayne know about the affair?" Bob asked.

"No, not as far as I can tell. Maybe Fern had told him and…"

"And you're putting him at the top of the suspect list, right?"

"Why not? It makes sense to me. What if she had broken

the news to him that night before going out with her friends?"

"Didn't she go directly from work?"

"Hmm... okay, you win that one in the observation stakes. Supposing she told him the night before and he was left at home, dwelling on it, got himself worked up into a state and abducted her."

"Possibly. What about the man at the pub and the black car? What car does Wayne drive?"

"There was a silver Merc sitting in the drive when we went to see him, I'm presuming that was his car. Get onto the station and run a check on that for me."

Bob made the call, and Claire answered the phone. He relayed the request and waited for her to work her magic on the system.

"Hi, Bob, yes, the car registered on Wayne Mitchell is a silver Merc. Do you need anything else?"

"Plenty, but it can wait until we get back. How are things going there?"

"They're heading in the right direction."

"We've got one more stop to make and then we'll be on our way back. Hang on." He turned to Sam and covered the phone. "Shall I tell them we'll bring lunch back with us?"

"Are you offering to pay?"

"Did I say that? Maybe I'll skip the idea instead."

"I'm teasing, they can all chip in when we get back. It probably won't be until around two. They might regard that as too long to wait."

"I'll ask. Hi, Claire, ask the others if they want us to pick up lunch on the way back, will you? It probably won't be until two or thereabouts."

"Sounds great to me. I'll ask the others and send the order through by text, how's that?"

"Yep, great stuff. See you later."

"There, that wasn't too hard, was it?" Sam grinned. "One good deed a day, I think that's going to be my objective from now on."

"Shit, really? That means I'll get roped into doing it as well."

"Not necessarily. Doesn't it make you feel all warm and fuzzy inside when you push the boat out and do a nice thing for someone?"

He hitched up a shoulder. "Can't say I've noticed, no."

CHAPTER 4

The receptionist at Westlands was a little off-hand to say the least when Sam asked if she could see Ivy Kitson. Sam had to assure her it was necessary and that they wouldn't be leaving until they had chatted with her. The woman had bristled and huffed and then left the area. She returned a few minutes later with another woman in her thirties, with short black hair. The newcomer seemed as agitated as the receptionist by the interruption to her day.

"You wanted to see me?" Ivy demanded authoritatively, although there was a note of uncertainty to her tone.

Sam produced her ID. "That's right, in private if possible. I'm DI Sam Cobbs, and this is my partner, DS Bob Jones."

Bob also showed his ID.

"May I ask what this is all about?"

Sam's gaze flipped between the receptionist and Ivy. "It would be better if we spoke privately."

"You've stated that already. I need to know why the police have the gall to turn up at my place of work, demanding to see me. Come on, spit it out."

"Very well. Against my better judgement, here goes: we're here to discuss your relationship with Fern Mitchell."

That did the trick. Ivy blushed despite it being quite cool in the hallway where they were standing. The receptionist's mouth dropped open.

"I... umm... I see. Yes, okay, we can discuss this matter in the staffroom. Thanks, Lynne, sorry to bother you." She dismissed the receptionist, who appeared to be glued in place, with a slight nudge.

"Oh, yes. Okay, I'll get back to work."

The receptionist bustled back behind her oak counter and pretended to shuffle papers while, Sam suspected, keeping one ear on anything that might be said as they made their way up the hallway. She was to be disappointed, though, as Ivy led the way in silence.

Sam and Bob shared fretful glances.

Ivy closed the door behind them and invited them to take a seat in the unoccupied room. "Why did you have to mention my relationship with Fern out there? It's likely to be all around the school by the end of the day."

"I apologise. I did my best to be discreet, but you forced my hand."

"Okay, I'm sorry, I shouldn't have done that. Why are you here? Have you found Fern? I'm guessing you have if you know about our affair. We did our utmost to keep it quiet, although Fern told me the week before she went missing that she had informed her best friends, the three ladies she was out with on that night."

"I'm going to come right out and tell you. Unfortunately, Fern's body was discovered this morning."

Ivy's eyes widened, and she repeatedly shook her head, all the time saying the word no, over and over.

"Would you like a drink of water?" Sam easily recognised the woman was in shock.

Ivy covered her face with her hands and openly sobbed.

Bob left his seat and filled a glass he found sitting on the draining board with cold water from the tap and placed it in front of Ivy. Sam smiled her appreciation for his thoughtfulness.

"When you feel up to it, Ivy, we have a few questions we'd like to ask you."

Ivy wiped her eyes on the sleeve of her jacket and said, "Like what? Wait, how did she die? I've been going out of my mind since she went missing last week. I've been out there, not with the others, but out there on my own, searching for her. To no avail. I didn't know where to look for the best or what to think. I've missed her so much since she's been gone, and now you're telling me that I'm never going to see her again."

"I'm sorry this has all come as such a shock to you. Fern was found in Derwentwater this morning."

"She was swimming? But she's an expert swimmer. There's no way she would have drowned. Maybe out at sea, but definitely not in a lake."

"She may have been a good swimmer but, I fear, circumstances were against her."

Ivy frowned and wiped away another stray tear. "What are you saying?"

"She was found fully clothed and, unfortunately, she had been shot."

Ivy leapt out of her chair and paced the area next to Sam. "What? Shot? I can't believe I'm hearing this. How has this been allowed to happen? We're not in America where guns are rife. As far as I know, there are very few guns on our streets. I can't get my head around this at all. For what purpose would anyone kidnap Fern only to end her life with a bullet? How is this even possible? God, I feel sick." Ivy rubbed her stomach with one hand and ran the other through her short spiky hair.

"Please try and remain calm. Getting yourself worked up into a state isn't going to achieve anything. We're interviewing those who were close to her to try to figure out how this has happened. Hence the reason we've come to see you today. Is there anything you can tell us about Fern? By that I mean, was she concerned about anything in particular lately?"

"You name it, she was worried about it. Fern was a born worrier."

"Was her husband aware of your affair?"

"No, she was supposed to have told him but assured me that the right opportunity hadn't presented itself. I was okay with that, I took a step back, not wanting to pressure her into doing something she wasn't comfortable with. I was happy sitting on the sidelines, seeing her when I could. The last thing I wanted was to force her into being with me, knowing that she might resent me later."

"You loved her?" Sam asked.

"With every breath I took. She was the most wonderful, caring human being to ever walk this planet, and now… she's gone and someone bloody killed her. Why? None of this makes any sense." She gasped and slapped a hand over her heart. "You don't suppose Wayne did this, do you?"

"We're unsure about that. Your affair has only just come to our attention. We'll need to question him further but, as far as you're concerned, he didn't know about your affair with his wife?"

"No. I'm sure she would have sent me a text message to tell me until we could discuss the issue in person, as it were. She didn't."

Sam nodded. "How long had you been together?"

"We were due to celebrate our four-month anniversary

last Saturday. I raised a glass in her absence, not knowing if she would ever return to me. Why would someone kill such a beautiful person? I know you're probably thinking the worst of her after learning about our affair but, honestly, our feelings were so powerful, it was impossible for either of us to resist. A love as fierce as ours was too difficult to ignore."

Sam had gone through similar feelings when she had met Rhys for the first time. Something deep inside had stirred and kept churning until they had finally kissed, empowering both of them. However, that had been after Chris had left the marital home. "I can understand that. What plans did the future hold for you both?"

"As soon as she told Wayne, she was going to move into my flat with me. We would have probably looked for a bigger place soon. That's never going to happen now, and I want to know why. Life can be so unfair at times. I've not had the best of years. My mother died of lung cancer, and my father is lost in the wilderness, not eating or caring for himself properly. Luckily, my sister lives just around the corner from him and agreed to move back home for a few months. That takes the pressure off me. I've also had a health scare this year, a cancer scare that tore my world apart, but I managed to overcome it with the love of my family and friends."

"I'm sorry you have had such a rough year. I'm sure Fern was a great source of comfort throughout the tough times."

"She was. Now she's gone, and I'm left with no one. Don't you know who did this?"

"No, not yet. In truth, our investigation only began a few hours ago. Did Fern ever mention to you that she was worried about anyone possibly following her, anything along those lines?"

"No, nothing at all, not that I can remember anyway."

"What about you? Have you come across anything out of the ordinary in your life recently?"

She shook her head, obviously deep in thought. "No, nothing."

"What about past lovers, could there be something there?"

"Not likely. My ex left the country six months ago and moved to Canada. Good riddance to her, too. She turned out to be an unstable, evil bitch."

"In what way?"

"The relationship started off well enough, but a few months in and I caught her checking my phone, showing up while I was out with my friends. Lack of trust, that sort of thing. I found it mind-boggling and unnerving. That's why I broke it off with her."

"Why Canada? Is she Canadian?"

"Nope, her family moved there ten years ago, and they've been pleading with her ever since to join them. Ending the relationship was the push she needed to finally hop on a plane and go out there."

"Do you have an address for her?"

"Why? She wouldn't be behind this," Ivy replied defensively.

"You stated that she was evil and unstable, she kind of fits the criteria for the person we're likely to be searching for."

"Shit! I never thought about that. I'm not sure if I've got it or not. I'll have to check my phone and it's in the classroom."

"It's okay, don't worry now. I'll leave you my card. You can text me the details later, if you would?"

"Of course. Damn, now you've brought it up, I can't get the image of her scowling face out of my mind. She was evil, she poisoned next door's cat because it kept coming into our garden. I went ballistic when I found out. That day signified the end of our disastrous relationship."

"Ouch, did the owner ever find out?"

"I think she suspected. She said it to me in passing once Tori had moved to Canada. I acted all innocent-like, not wishing to get involved. But it sickened me to think Tori had taken her foul mood out on an innocent animal."

"Shocking behaviour. Tori what?"

"Sinclair."

"We can check the airlines, see if anyone of that name has arrived in the UK in the last week or so."

"Sounds like a good idea. Although, if she were here, I think she would have been pounding on my door before now."

"We'll check, all the same. Anything else you can think of?"

She stared off into the corner for a few moments. "No, not really. Tell me you're going to be looking closely at Wayne. They had a tempestuous marriage. All wasn't as rosy as he often made out around here. Once I got to know the real Fern, I realised that the stories he told about their marriage, during breaks in the staffroom, were mostly made up."

"Why would he do that?"

Ivy shrugged. "To cover up the fact that their marriage was on the rocks, I guess. No one likes to admit they're a failure, do they?"

"I suppose. There's no chance he was having an affair, is there?"

"I don't think so. If he was, Fern didn't know, otherwise she would have used that as an excuse to get out of the marriage."

"We'll do some digging. Okay, we're going to leave you to it now. Our condolences for your loss. Here's my card. If you can send Tori's details through at your earliest convenience, that would be wonderful."

"Within the next half an hour, I promise. Please, do all you can to find who did this to Fern. I don't think it has properly sunk in yet. It'll probably hit me hard at the end of the day."

"Take care. You have my assurance that we'll go above and beyond during the investigation. It never sits comfortably with coppers, knowing that there is a killer on the loose, brandishing a dangerous weapon."

"I can believe it. Thank you for coming here today to break the news to me in person."

"You're welcome."

Ivy showed them back to the main entrance just as Wayne Mitchell walked through the front door. He stopped mid-stride, his gaze darting between Ivy, Sam and Bob.

"Inspector, I wasn't expecting to see you here."

"Just following up on a few enquiries, Mr Mitchell. How are you?"

"Not too bad, considering I was told this morning that my wife had been murdered. How would you expect me to feel?"

"Sorry. Well, we must go. Thanks for speaking with us, Miss Kitson."

"May I ask why you spoke to her?" Mitchell demanded, his eyes narrowing with suspicion.

"We're not at liberty to disclose that, sir. It's all part of our enquiry."

He glared at Sam through narrow slits. "I'm aware of what's going on, I just wondered if either of you had the guts to tell me."

Bob took a step towards him. "All right, sir. Tone it down a bit."

"Why should I? Why wasn't I told this bitch was having an affair with my wife? Why is it always the husband that is the last to know?"

"Don't talk daft, Wayne," Ivy said.

"How did you find out?" Sam asked.

He pointed at the receptionist sitting behind the desk.

"Mouth almighty over there. Tell her a secret and it'll be halfway round Cumbria within the hour."

Sam admonished the receptionist with a disgruntled glare. She lowered her head and shuffled some papers to avoid any further confrontation. "I'm sorry you found out this way."

"Would you have told me?" he asked Sam.

"Eventually."

"What about her, is she a suspect? Is that why you've come to see her? Did she kill my wife?"

"Don't be so ridiculous, Wayne, why would I kill the woman I loved more than life itself?"

"Bullshit! How can you stand there and profess to know what love is when the person you had fallen for was already happily married?"

Ivy crossed her arms over her flat chest. "Happily married, is that some kind of joke? Your marriage was rockier than a boat stuck out in a violent storm, struggling to stay upright in the turbulent ocean."

"You believe what you want to believe. I can categorically tell you there was nothing wrong with our marriage."

"If you tell yourself that often enough you might begin to believe it. Your marriage was dead in the water. It was only a matter of time before Fern packed her bags and moved in with me."

Sam inched between the warring pair. "Please stop this. Don't do this here, not now, when you're both grieving. It's not right, and you're likely to regret the words you say in anger."

"I'm not. And yes, I'm grieving, I have a right to grieve because she belonged to *me*, she was my wife." Wayne stomped his foot on the marble floor, emphasising his point.

"Hark at him. She belonged to *no one*, she was a free spirit.

She didn't love you, she loved me," Ivy insisted, tears glistening in her dark-brown pixie-like eyes.

"She wasn't a lesbian. We had an active sex life, there's no way she would—"

Sam raised a hand to silence them. "Let's not say anything we're likely to regret. Do you really want to do this publicly?"

There was a small crowd gathering. Luckily, most of the students were still stuck in the classrooms. The people milling around were older, possibly teachers or even student teachers.

Bob turned and did his best to disperse the crowd. "Nothing to see here, ladies and gents. On your way now. Thank you."

Ivy placed a hand on each of her hips. "I'm willing to thrash it out with him, if that's what he wants. He'll come out the loser. But if he wants to air his dirty laundry in public, then bring it on."

Sam sighed. "I wouldn't advise either of you saying anything else to inflame the situation. Let things settle down, then if you want to have a conversation with each other, I would suggest you do it on mutual ground, away from the school. But please, not yet, not while all this is so raw for you both. It's obvious that Fern cared a lot about each of you. Can't you leave it there?"

"I can't, no. I want this sorted out here and now," Wayne asserted. "That's why I've come down here, to have it out with her."

"Fair enough. Where? Here is fine with me."

"Please, the pair of you, you're going to regret this. At least take it into the staffroom," Sam insisted. She glanced at Bob and rolled her eyes.

He did the same in return.

Ivy didn't say another word. She turned and walked back towards the staffroom with Wayne close behind her.

"Shit! Not what we need right now, eh, boss?"

"Just what I was thinking, Bob. God help us. It's likely to get feisty in there. Stay alert in case one of them lashes out at the other."

"Pistols drawn at dawn type of thing. Oh joy, something to look forward to."

"I could have done without you mentioning a gun, matey, but yes, stay alert."

Inside the staffroom, Sam positioned the angry couple a few feet apart and ordered them to sit, ensuring there was a table between the four of them for safety.

"Who wants to go first?" Sam asked.

"Me. How did it start, your *dirty little affair*?" Wayne demanded.

"Umm… let's try and keep things civil at all times," Sam said, her patience already wearing thin.

"She came to see you one day. We bumped into each other in the hallway and… it was love at first sight."

"That's sick. You knew she was married to me. Why go after her?"

"We couldn't help ourselves. There was an instant attraction that neither of us could deny. We didn't intend it to happen."

"Did you try to stop it?"

"No, why should I? It takes two to tango," Ivy snapped back.

Sam imagined the blood boiling in Wayne's veins.

"You're nothing but a home-breaking slut," he said.

Sam raised her hand again. If she had a bell, she would have used it to call time out between them. "Less of the insults. I appreciate how uncomfortable this situation must be for both of you, but try and respect each other's emotional state at this sad time."

"Emotional state? I'm grieving because I've lost the one

perfect thing in my life and have no hope of getting her back," Wayne said. He ran a hand through his hair and let it drop heavily on the table.

"The last thing I want is for us to be at each other's throat," Ivy told him. "We're going to need to put our heads together over the next week or two, so it would be better if we could get along."

Both Sam and Bob frowned, but it was the grieving husband who asked the obvious question. "What are you going on about, you insane bitch?"

Sam pointed at him. "I won't warn you again, Mr Mitchell."

He didn't get a chance to apologise because Ivy leapt in and said, "To organise the funeral. We'll need to do that together. It's what Fern would have wanted."

Bugger, now she's lit the touchpaper. Sam raised an eyebrow at Bob, warning him to be prepared.

"Fuck off!" Wayne stood, tipping his chair back. "You're not going to be involved in the preparations. That's going to be down to me. She was my wife, not yours. Go fucking screw yourself with your bloody dildo, woman. You women make me laugh. Can't be doing with a man but you still use a pretend prick to satisfy yourselves."

Sam flinched at the callousness behind his attack. "Mr Mitchell, I've asked you on more than one occasion not to get personal with your confrontations. One more time, and I'll be forced to arrest you."

"Don't be so absurd, you can't do that."

Ivy leapt to her feet and retaliated, "Ha, at least a rubber penis is able to satisfy a woman when most men can't!"

"Ivy you're making matters worse," Sam warned.

Bob flew out of his chair and approached Mitchell. "She's quite within her rights to arrest you. Now sit down and calm down, or I'll march you out of here and make a show of you in front of the rest of the teachers and the pupils as well. Is that what you want?"

Sam's pride in her partner intensified at that moment. She felt like standing up and giving Bob a round of applause. They had both jumped in when necessary. For now, the situation seemed less tense as Ivy and Wayne returned to their seats.

"If we could try and keep things under control. This isn't an easy position for anyone to have to contend with, but you're both going to have to make an effort to get along, considering what lies ahead of you," Sam was quick to advise them.

"I can't believe I'm hearing this. You're siding with her, aren't you? You think she has a right to swan in and help organise *my* wife's funeral? Well, I've got news for both of you, I'll employ a solicitor and take her to court rather than sit back and let that happen," Wayne shouted, his arms crossing in defiance.

"I wasn't saying anything of the sort, however, for everyone's sake, I think it might be wise to get together and make the arrangements, if only to lower each of your stress levels. From what I have gathered, Fern loved both of you. I'm sure she'll be up there, looking down on you, willing you to get along for long enough to organise her funeral."

"I agree," Ivy said.

"You would," Wayne replied. "My threat still stands. You're going nowhere near my wife's body, you hear me? She's mine, and I will give her the sendoff she deserves."

"How can I sit here and listen to such codswallop? Fern was intending to leave you. Why can't you get that through that thick skull of yours?"

"I have your word on that and your word only. So you can fucking go to hell. Excuse my language, but you've driven me to this. I'm usually a calm, assertive man."

Ivy snorted. "Of course you are, in your bloody dreams. I've heard you shouting at the kids in your class when I've walked past your door. Plus, I know of several incidents which have taken place at home where you've raised a hand to Fern when things have got heated between you."

"Hearsay, that would never stand up in court. Tell her, Inspector."

Sam shook her head. "Keep me out of it. Look, we're going to need to leave soon, you know, we have a killer to find, in case either of you had forgotten. I'd like to think that I could trust you not to tear strips out of each other when we leave."

"There's no need for you to search any further," Ivy replied. "The killer is sitting opposite me."

"What? You're frigging insane. How many times do I have to tell you? I loved my wife."

"Okay, I think we need to bring this conversation to a halt, let you both reassess things and allow your emotions time to come to terms with the loss you've suffered, then, maybe you can meet up again when things aren't so raw," Sam suggested.

"It's not going to happen. I'm not in the habit of repeating myself. I've given my reasons why, and they still stand. I won't be changing my mind on the subject, ever," Wayne said adamantly.

"Ignorant sod," Ivy muttered and left her chair. She headed towards the door and flung over her shoulder, "I have a friend who is a solicitor. I'll run it past her and get back to you with the outcome."

"Don't hold your breath, sweetheart. I think you'll find the law is on my side. Signing a marriage certificate is like signing a contract. It's a shame other people don't comprehend that."

Sam and Bob shared a bemused look and attempted to leave the room after Ivy, but Wayne had another idea.

"Thanks for backing me up throughout that conversation. I thought better of you, Inspector."

"First of all, Mr Mitchell, you barely know me, so you have no right to judge me. Secondly, I did what is expected of me. I did my damnedest to keep the peace between two people who obviously loved the victim. For what it's worth, I think you're wrong treating Ivy the way you have, but that's a personal and not a professional opinion."

"Then I shall ignore it. Only your professional advice matters to me right now. Goodbye, Inspector, don't forget to update me with any news you receive regarding my wife's death, as and when you obtain it."

"Don't worry, I won't. We'll be in touch soon."

Sam and Bob left the staffroom. Ivy was nowhere to be seen in the hallway. They made their way past the inquisitive and interfering receptionist to outside the building where Sam sucked in several deep breaths of fresh air.

"Jesus, what is wrong with people?"

"Umm... I'm on the fence with this one, boss. I think they're both in an invidious position, damned if they do and damned if they don't."

"I hear you. Still, hopefully it won't become an issue that we need to deal with again in the near future. Let's get lunch sorted and return to the station, not that I have much appetite left after dealing with that shit."

CHAPTER 5

Friday

It was time. He'd held the woman for the last two days, since he'd killed the first one. This bitch had been feisty from the word go and had driven him nuts. He'd endeavoured to inhibit her feistiness, but nothing had worked so far. He'd tried not feeding her, because on one occasion she had thrown the food in his face. He wasn't one to let things lie and had taken the greatest of pleasure reprimanding her for her sins. Teaching her to obey him when all she wanted to do was fight and take flight.

However, once the initial shock of what he'd done to her had diminished, her feistiness had returned with a vengeance, hence the need for him to rid himself of the burden.

After he had abducted her, she told him that she recognised him, but she struggled to place how or where. She had pleaded with him to tell her, but he had refused. It added an extra thrill to the encounter to keep his captives guessing. They wouldn't succeed, he'd always been someone others regarded as a nobody, someone lingering at the back of the room with little to say on any subject. He'd had that beaten into him when he was barely out of nappies by his wicked father. His mother had died whilst giving life to him, and his father had never stopped punishing him for her untimely death. His father had loved her with a passion, so he'd repeatedly told him during every torturous lesson he had given him over the years.

Why him? He had no other siblings for his father to vent his anger on, maybe that was why he was open to be vilified and degraded daily. His upbringing had been the foundation for everything else in his life thus far. Once he'd left school and started earning a living, although his father had stolen most of his wages at the end of each month, he did his best to join as many clubs as possible. The main purpose being, to feel involved. He'd lived a life of solitude, often locked in his bedroom for hours on end, waiting for his father to remember to feed him. A bowl of soup here and a sandwich made with mouldy bread there had been his salvation and what had kept him alive most months. The social workers were useless, they had put his skinny legs and arms down to him outgrowing his body, his rapid growth spurts. It was no such thing. Beneath the layers of clothes he wore in order to keep warm was the proof that barely any food touched his lips, ever.

He shuddered at the image that emerged, the day he thought he was going to die through lack of food. It had been the day his father had cooked himself a roast dinner and left it lying on the table while he'd nipped to the toilet. Marco had managed to unnail his window and shimmy down the drainpipe. He'd snuck in through the open back door and tucked in to his father's dinner, shovelling it down his neck at the speed of light. After a few mouthfuls, he had to resist the urge to be sick, his stomach objecting to the richness of the food passing his lips.

His father had come back into the room and beaten him until he was black and blue, breaking his arm and one of his legs in the process. Marco had cried out, begged for mercy. His father had shown him mercy by taking him to hospital and telling the doctor that he had found his son lying in the road outside his house, beaten up by a gang who had robbed him of his pocket money. The police were called in. His father had a quiet word in his ear, warning him what would happen if he didn't play along with the lie.

That day, Marco had felt nothing but compassion from the people dealing with his injuries. It dawned on him what an utterly miserable existence he'd been living and vowed to change it, eventually.

"When are you going to let me go?" his captive whimpered.

He struck her face, hard, sending her head snapping to the side with a force he didn't realise he possessed. He should have, after what he'd carried out over the past few months, but he lacked any belief in his own capabilities and often surprised himself. "Shut up. How many more times do I have to tell you to keep that mouth of yours shut? Do you want me to put the gag on you again?"

"No, please. I promise I'll be quiet."

"Good. Anyway, in an hour or so, we are going to take a ride out."

"To where? Can I go home now?"

He watched the hope and expectancy rise in her eyes and, to counter it, with a clenched fist, he lashed out again, twice. Her head whipped first one way and then the other in quick succession. The bones in her neck crunched, complaining against the viciousness of the attack.

He bent down to her level and sneered, "What did I tell you?"

She turned her head away and sniffled, having the sense not to utter an apology.

He beamed, satisfied by the reaction he was provoking in her. She was scared of him, terrified of what he was about to do to her, and with good reason. He knew what lay ahead of them. It was early, only five-thirty in the morning, still dark outside, an ideal day for her life to end, and it would, sooner rather than later.

"Get up on your feet."

"I need to go to the bathroom. I won't be able to hold on much longer."

Marco pushed her along the hallway to the old Victorian-style bathroom with its claw footed bath and toilet cistern positioned high up on the wall.

"Can you untie me?"

"No," he shouted and tore down her jeans and panties, then he pushed her onto the toilet seat.

She stared at him. "Can you give me some privacy?"

"Nope. Get on with it. The clock is ticking, and you have thirty seconds to complete your business before we leave."

Her brow wrinkled in concentration. Eventually, she rid herself of the extra load in her body. "Can I wipe myself?"

He nodded and turned away.

"I'm finished now, thank you."

He yanked up her panties and her jeans and then stopped at the sink long enough for her to rinse her hands. He dried them on the towel and then shoved her out into the hallway and down the stairs. The car was parked outside. He sat her in the front seat, not bothered if anyone would see her. He'd been watching the news religiously, and there had been no talk of her going missing, much to his relief.

They set off, their destination around thirty minutes

away. It was still dark at this time of year. The trees swayed in the wind that had picked up overnight. Was there a storm brewing? He hoped not, not for what he had in mind for later.

The destination rose ahead of them. The long drive down was extremely narrow and winding in places. It peaked and dipped at times, but the magnificence of their surroundings wasn't lost on him. He adored this place. It was where he liked to hang out the most. Time passed slowly when he was here, exploring the many footpaths branching off from the fabulous lake. The lake he had spent many an hour bobbing around, the ice-cold water sending a thrill to his brain and extremities. He knew it intimately, every shelf on the bed and every nook and cranny around its edges. The branches and boulders under the surface were capable of damaging many a boat testing the waters.

He pulled into his regular parking spot, close to the edge of the water, and unpacked the inflatable boat from the boot, keeping her in the car, her hands tied. He made certain she couldn't get away by locking the doors while he set up.

Once the boat was swaying as the gentle waves lapped the shoreline on the man-made beach, he tied the rope around one of the large boulders and went back to the car to fetch her.

"Are you going to behave, or do I have to gag you?"

"I'll be good. Do anything you want me to do."

"Glad to hear it. Get out."

He hoisted her out of the car, and they descended the couple of steps which led down to the boat.

"What are we doing here? It's too dark to see."

"Nothing wrong with your eyesight, despite the black eye I gave you for pissing me off earlier. You won't do that again in a hurry, will you?"

"No, I promised you I wouldn't try anything else. I've learnt my lesson..."

"I have ways of making people listen to me."

"I know."

He grinned. "You shouldn't have been so reluctant. Learning fast to obey me could have saved all this hassle."

She nodded, and her chin dipped to her chest and settled there until he yanked on her arm and tugged her into the boat. It wasn't much of a vessel, but it would serve its purpose and get them from A to B.

"Get in the boat."

"Why?" she asked.

It turned out to be a foolish question, and he aimed a heavy punch to her stomach. She doubled over. He held on to her arm, preventing her from falling to the ground. Then he assisted her into the boat. He climbed aboard himself, picked up the oars and rowed around the small island of pine trees in the centre of the lake. There, where he knew the water was deeper, he ceased rowing.

"What are we doing out here?"

Her eyes widened in the darkness, and she peered over her shoulder at the shoreline that was around fifty feet away.

"Don't even think about swimming back either. I have something special planned for you, my lovely."

She cringed. It was obvious he made her skin crawl. Well, that feeling wouldn't last. It would all be over soon, for her.

The boat rocked unsteadily when he stood. "Oops, silly me, I need to be more careful. Wouldn't want either one of us falling in now, would I?"

She swallowed noisily. "I have no idea what your intentions are..."

"You're going to find out soon enough." He laughed and sat again.

She searched around her.

He sensed she was about to call out for help and kicked her leg. "Don't think about screaming either."

"I wasn't going to. Please, I'm cold, can't we go now?"

"What have I told you about keeping that mouth of yours shut?"

"I'm sorry," yet another mumbled apology left her quivering lips.

"You will be."

He pounced, and before she had the chance to realise what was happening, he'd lifted her from her seat and dropped her over the side, into the water. She attempted to scream. His fist connected with her mouth, hitting her harder than he'd anticipated. Her head lolled to the side. He had hold of her jacket by the collar with one hand, and with the other, splashed water in her face to revive her.

She spluttered and thrashed, her tied hands restricting her movements. "Please, get me out of here. I'm freezing. I'm going to die."

"Bravo, it's finally sinking in—forgive the pun there." He laughed.

The boat rocked from side to side the more she panicked. He'd had enough. His intentions were to string out her death, to prolong her suffering, but now, all he wanted to do was get it over and done with.

He placed his free hand firmly on the top of her head and pushed down, forcing her under the water. Bubbles quickly materialised and then died down. He removed his hand and allowed her to bob to the surface. She inhaled a large breath. He thrust her under the water again. The bitch had tried to fool him into believing she was already dead. She couldn't outwit him. He would continue to hold her under. The bubbles dispersed yet again, and he removed his hand from her head. She broke through the surface of the still water.

This time, her eyes were wide open in a death stare. He placed two fingers to her neck. No pulse. She was dead.

He left her floating and made his way back to the shore. He cleaned up the area, ensuring he didn't leave any clues lying around for forensics to find. He bolted back to the car and headed home, to the cottage.

Another bitch taken care of.

CHAPTER 6

"Jesus, not another one. I can't believe this is happening," Sam complained above the sound of the siren she had switched on to combat the heavy traffic, caused by the new roadworks on the outskirts of Workington.

"All right, calm down. Hey, watch that comedian, he's trying to come out of the road up ahead. Steady on, boss."

"What? He shouldn't be in the bloody way, so what if I scared the shit out of him?"

"Not only him," Bob muttered. He folded his arms and then just as quickly unfolded them again to cling to the seat.

Sam weaved in and out of the traffic when an opening arose on the other side of the road. Eventually, the swarm of vehicles eased, and she switched off the siren to continue the rest of the journey. It took them just over half an hour to reach Buttermere where Des had requested their immediate attendance.

She drew the car to a halt behind one of the SOCO vans. "We'd better suit up."

Bob strained his neck to look out of the side window and pointed. "They're down there, by the lake."

"No shit, Sherlock, where else would they be?"

"All right, there's no need to be sarcastic."

After pulling on protective suits and signing the Crime Scene Log, they trotted down the few steps and onto the man-made beach to join Des and the rest of his team.

"Morning, Des." Sam checked her watch, wondering if it was afternoon yet. The call had come in from the pathologist at around eleven-ten. It was now five minutes to midday. The traffic had held them up more than Sam had realised.

"Only just, I believe. What kept you? No, don't answer that, I've heard enough bloody excuses from members of my team today to last me a lifetime. You're here now, finally. Let's call that a result and be grateful for small mercies, eh?"

"I'm not getting into a row with you. I always do my utmost to get to a crime scene as quickly as is humanly possible. If I could grow wings, it would probably make life a hell of a lot easier. Unfortunately, I can't."

"I thought you said you were going to avoid getting into a row with me. Calm down, Inspector. Living on the edge all the time can be detrimental to your health."

"I am; and I'm not," Sam replied, confusing herself as well as those around her. "What have we got here?"

"That young man over there arrived for a morning swim this morning. He discovered the body of the victim. A female in her early thirties. No other major injuries on her, so I'm presuming she was drowned."

"On purpose?"

Des raised an eyebrow. "How many people do you know who prefer to go swimming fully clothed?"

"Ouch, okay. My head is still stuck in the traffic. I apologise for my obvious slip-up." She glanced at the body of the victim. It wasn't bloated, not to that extent. "She hasn't been in the water that long, has she?"

"That's correct. I would say no longer than a couple of hours maximum."

"Are we connecting the two crimes at this stage?"

Des inhaled a large breath and studied the victim. "Let's look at the evidence we can see without carrying out a PM. Two women, both dying in lakes, one shot and one perhaps purposefully drowned. No matter which way you view the second victim, I'd still be inclined to call it murder at this stage. So, take from that what you will."

"Connected then," Bob said.

Des applauded him. "Give that man a gold medal for observation."

Bob glanced at Sam who averted her gaze with a smirk.

"Both *young* women at that," Sam added. "Okay, we'll have a word with the person who found her." She pointed to a man who had a foil blanket around his shoulders.

"You do that. I asked him to hang around, knew you'd be wanting a word in his shell-like."

"We'll get that out of the way now and come back to see you afterwards."

Sam and Bob removed their overalls and deposited them in the waiting black bag, then they picked their way across the pebbled beach to the witness.

Sam produced her ID and introduced herself and Bob. "Thank you for waiting to see us, Mr…?"

"Strong, Adam Strong. I never expected to discover a dead body down here. Well, you wouldn't, would you? It was a bloody shock, I can tell you."

"Where did you find her?"

"Around the other side of the island there. I usually swim round it a couple of times to warm up before I do my lengths, if that makes sense?"

"It does. What time did you arrive here this morning?"

"The same time I always do, at six forty-five. I come every morning, or try to, swim for forty-five minutes, then go home, jump in the shower, and then head off to work."

"I'm presuming it was still dark at that time of the morning. Did you see anyone else down here?"

"Yes, I arrived at the same time a couple of walkers set off up the hills there, along that path. We parked in the large space at the top."

"Were there any other cars around at the time?"

"None that I noticed, no."

"What about on your journey here? The road is quite narrow, did you have to pull over to let anyone pass?"

"No, not today. Other days I have to, now and again, there are always a few delivery drivers around at that time of the morning, you know, dropping off supplies to the pub or cafés up the road. But nothing at all this morning. But there are other roads out of here, it's not like this is the only route in and out of this place."

"You read my mind, I was thinking the same. Have you seen the two walkers come back?"

"Yes, they returned to their car around an hour later and drove off. Can I go now? My veins are like blocks of ice. I've been standing around here for hours."

"Of course. If we can get your details, we'll need to drop by and see you, to take down a proper statement, at your convenience."

"Fine by me, just not today. I'm going to need to make up the time I've lost this morning when I get back to work. The boss is like a mini Hitler if he thinks the staff are taking the piss."

"Oh? Where do you work?"

"At a medical supply outlet about five miles from here. Thrilling work, packing boxes all day long."

Sam smiled. "Maybe something better will come along soon."

"I doubt it. I always wanted to be a copper, but my fitness levels weren't up to scratch when I applied. That's why I started swimming, to get fit. Never bloody dreamed it would lead to me discovering a body in the lake."

"Sorry you've had that experience. Hey, don't let it put you off applying for the force again. We're always on the lookout for capable recruits joining us."

His head waved from side to side. "I'm not sure. Maybe I'll do it next year, not sure I'm fit enough right now."

He gave Bob his address, and then Sam and Bob walked away.

"Poor bloke was really shaken up," Bob said. "He's a darn sight fitter than me. He should get in if he's that fit."

"Yeah, he seems fit enough to me." Sam wiggled her eyebrows and smiled. "I'm guessing this incident has changed his mind. I remember laying eyes on my first dead body, it wasn't a pleasant experience. I had to give myself a good talking-to when I got home that night."

"What are you saying? That you almost quit the force?" Bob frowned.

"I can't lie, the thought crossed my mind."

"Christ, that would have been a great loss."

Sam smiled. "Why thank you, kind sir."

They returned to where Des and his team were working but remained ten feet away so they didn't have to tog up again.

"Anything else for us, Des?" Sam asked.

"Such as? Bearing in mind I'll be performing the PM later and that's usually where I discover what truly happened to the victim."

"Sorry I asked," Sam mumbled.

Bob sniggered beside her, earning a sharp dig in the ribs.

"Okay, I'll speak to you later. We'll get on with the investigation for now."

"Good luck with that. There was no ID on her, you forgot to ask."

"I didn't. I knew you would have mentioned it if there had been."

He glanced up to look at her and raised his eyebrows.

"Come on, Bob, let's get out of here before I lose my rag with him. He's being mighty insufferable today."

"Ooo… hark at you. Swallowed a dictionary for breakfast along with your porridge, did you?"

"I can come out with the big words when it suits, you cheeky git."

"Where are we going to begin on this one?"

"The most obvious place. Miss Pers. If we're dealing with the same killer, he kept the first victim locked away somewhere for a week. The odds are he did the same with this victim."

"Ah, yes, you might be right. Want me to get the ball rolling in the car en route?"

"Makes sense to me."

They climbed the steps again, and Sam stared off into the distance, surveying the area, trying to work out in which direction the killer left. "This is the road we came in on, and back that way is the road leading on to Honister Pass, right?"

"Correct. It's a possibility he chose to leave that way. Depends on where he came from and what his destination was."

"I wish we knew." She got in the car and brought up the map on the satnav screen. "I think too many variables are on the table. There are far too many towns up ahead for us to choose from."

"There's no point in us trying." Bob withdrew his mobile from his jacket pocket and rang the station, putting it on speaker. "Hi, Claire…, yeah, it's me. We've got another female, death by drowning, suspected foul play. No ID found at the scene, so we're wandering around blind at the moment. The boss wants us to check with Missing Persons."

"Want me to flip through the more recent notifications?" Claire asked.

"If you wouldn't mind. The first victim was held for a week before she showed up. Go back as far as last Friday, no, make it Thursday, will you?"

"I'll crack on with that now and see what I can come up with. I'll get back to you soon."

"We'll take a leisurely drive back, admire the scenery. Thanks, Claire."

"It's all right for some." Claire laughed and hung up.

"Since when do we have a leisurely drive anywhere?" Sam asked with an added tut.

"Worth a try. Our working day is usually carried out at breakneck speed. I just thought it would make a change, that's all."

"There's a reason for that, Bob."

"Wishful thinking on my part then, how's that?"

"More like it. We'll take the same route back, although it's bound to be busier at this time of the day."

They had only travelled a few miles up the winding roads when Claire rang back. At the same time Bob's mobile signalled that a text had come through. He put the phone on speaker again. "Hi, Claire, you're on speaker. What have you got for us?"

"I've sent you a text with a photo of a young woman who has been reported missing since Wednesday. Here's the thing that jumped out at me: she was reported missing after going for a swim at Derwentwater."

"What? On Wednesday, the day we found the first victim's body?" Sam asked incredulously.

"So it would seem, ma'am. The timeline matches as well. She always prefers to swim early in the morning."

"Jesus, so the killer must have hung around and picked her up at the same time he killed victim one, is that what we're saying?" Bob chipped in.

Sam indicated and pulled over. "Let me see the photo, Bob."

He scrolled through his phone and nodded. "It's her, I'm sure it is." He angled the phone in Sam's direction.

"Yep, I agree. We're going to need her address and the contact details of the person who reported her missing, Claire."

"Sending that to Bob now."

Her partner's phone pinged again. "I've got it. Thanks."

"Good work, Claire. We'll head over there now and be in touch soon."

"Good luck," Claire said and ended the call.

THEY DROVE to the address which was roughly equidistant from the two crime scenes. The house was a mid-terrace in a row of five on a new large estate.

"Stay here, I'll see if anyone is at home first." Sam left the car and rang the doorbell.

The door remained unanswered. She stood back on the pavement and checked the upstairs windows. There was no movement up there from what she could tell. So she decided to check with the neighbour. A young woman came to the door holding a toddler with a toy car close to his mouth.

"Hello, what can I do for you?"

Sam presented her warrant card. "Sorry to disturb you. I'm trying to track down your neighbour, Lee McCoy. Have you seen him lately?"

"I shouldn't think so, he works during the day. You'll find

him at the garage up the road, he's a mechanic there. Has he done something wrong?"

"No, it's nothing like that. Thanks very much for your help, sorry to trouble you."

"It's okay. It's nice to see someone different during the day. It's usually only me and Tommy, and the cartoons on TV, of course."

Sam smiled and waved farewell. She jumped back in the car and started the engine. "He's a mechanic up the road. We'll catch up with him there."

The garage turned out to be a stone's throw from the house.

"Blimey, talk about working on your doorstep," Bob commented.

"Not sure if that's a good or bad thing, depends if he owns the business or not."

"I suppose."

They left the vehicle and entered the workshop. Two mechanics over on the left were eating their lunch while having a laugh. In the pit there was a solitary mechanic working on one of the cars.

Sam approached the two men on the left. "Hi, I'm looking for Lee McCoy. Is he around?"

"Macca, there's a lady to see you, mate," the older male shouted at the mechanic working under the car.

"Thanks," Sam replied.

She and Bob moved away from the two men and waited for Lee to join them at the end of a workbench.

She offered up her ID and said, "Hi, Lee, I'm DI Sam Cobbs, and this is my partner, DS Bob Jones. Is there somewhere private where we can have a chat?"

The man, his face covered in grease, frowned and asked, "Oh, I see. Is this about Anna?"

Sam nodded. "It is. Do you have an office where we

could go?"

"Over here. The boss is out at the moment. I'm sure he won't mind us talking in there."

Sam followed him over to the office which had a glass wall on the right.

He wiped his hands on an oil-stained cloth and used the brass handle to open the door. "I won't ask you to sit as I feel like an intruder as it is. What news do you have for me?"

"I'm sorry, it's not good news. We discovered what we believe to be Anna's body in Buttermere Lake this morning."

He sank onto the desk behind him and leapt to his feet again. "Shit, I shouldn't have done that. Bugger, I wasn't expecting you to say that. Jesus! How did she die?"

"She drowned. Another swimmer discovered her at first light this morning."

"Impossible. She's a superb swimmer, she has never got into difficulty before. I used to liken her to a mermaid, she was always more at home in the water than on dry land. Shit! I can't believe she's gone." He wiped a hand around his face.

"I'm so sorry for your loss. Are you up to answering a few questions for us?"

"If I have to. Not sure if I'll have the answers you're after, though. Christ, what am I going to tell her mother? She's only just lost her father to cancer, barely six weeks ago."

"That's awful, I'm sorry."

"It's not your fault. God, her mother is a complete wreck, this news is likely to finish her off. Not sure I could deal with that being on my conscience. Shit, how selfish am I? Sorry, just ignore me. I'll dig deep and ask the boss for some time off work and do the deed later."

"If you'd rather we broke the news to her, I'm not averse to doing that for you."

"Thanks. I think it would be less of a shock coming from me. Who am I trying to kid? It doesn't matter, I'll deal with it later. What questions do you have?" He covered his face with both of his hands and shook his head. He dropped his hands and stared Sam in the eye. "This is bloody incredible. Drowned, I can't believe it. Not Anna, she had fins instead of arms. Sorry to go on, but she was a natural born swimmer. I can't imagine her getting into trouble."

Sam chewed on the inside of her lip and then revealed the truth. "We believe it was foul play."

"Meaning? No… you think she was killed? Someone deliberately drowned her?"

"So it would seem. She was fully clothed when she died."

He frowned again. "As opposed to wearing a wetsuit?"

"Yes. Can you tell us when she went missing?"

"Wednesday, early morning. She frequently goes to Derwentwater to swim first thing. She used to say it set her up for the day. Most times she went in with just her costume on, but when the weather was too bad, she got togged up in a wetsuit, but she didn't really like it. Much preferred to feel the water on her skin. The cold livened up her nerve endings she used to tell me. You wouldn't catch me in the water, not at the times of year she went in. The sun has to be blistering hot before I attempt to dip even a toe."

"I'm the same." Bob glanced up from the notes he was taking.

"Do you know at what time she went to Derwent?"

"Around six-thirty, I suppose. I shot down there on Wednesday to see if I could find her. I found the car, but there was no sign of her. I have a spare key for the car. Her handbag and phone were both inside, but her clothes were missing."

"So she had got changed then? What about her swimming costume or wetsuit, was that in the car?"

"Yes, her costume and wet towel were in the boot, in a bag. That's why I rang the cop shop, sorry, the station, right away. But they fobbed me off, told me that I needed to file a Missing Person report after she had been missing twenty-four hours. The thing is, I instinctively knew that something was wrong and yet I couldn't get anyone down at the station to listen to me. I was treated appallingly."

"So sorry you had such a bad experience. It's true, we can't act upon a missing person report until twenty-four hours have passed, but there are ways of saying things. You should never have been dealt with like that. I'll have a word with the duty sergeant upon our return. Did you happen to get the name of the officer you spoke to?"

"I didn't. It was a youngish bloke, judging by his voice. Anyway, that day turned out to be nightmarish for me. I couldn't face coming in to work. I drove around for hours, trying to find her. I wondered if she might have hit her head and wandered off somewhere. Daft really, but I suppose I was clutching at straws. Your mind plays tricks on you when you can't function right."

"And you rang the station again yesterday morning, is that correct?"

"Yes, I put the call in at around eight, just to be sure. It's a stupid rule, you need to revisit it, especially now she's shown up dead."

"I agree. I'll pass on your concerns to my senior officers."

"Like that's going to make a difference."

Sam smiled and shrugged. "It might do, some day. Did an officer come out and speak with you?"

"No, it was all handled over the phone. The woman I spoke to apologised for the way I had been treated and put it down to a massive investigation that was taking place in the area. That night, on the news, I heard a report about a woman being shot at Derwentwater. You'd think someone would have twigged, wouldn't you? I'm not being stupid, am I? Could they be connected? You know, a woman shot by a sniper and my girlfriend going missing at the very same place, on the exact same day?"

"We're investigating both crimes, and yes, we have come to the conclusion that both murders have possibly been committed by the same killer."

He sat back on the desk again but this time remained there. The recent high colour in his cheeks that had been visible behind the grease suddenly paled, and he stared at the floor. "Jesus, this is so bloody hard to take in. The last thing I expected to hear. Do you think the killer knew who she was?"

"Possibly. We won't know the answer to that until we start digging. Did your girlfriend know the first victim, Fern Mitchell?"

He shrugged, and his upturned hands crashed onto his thighs. "I don't know. I didn't recognise the name, you know, when they mentioned it on the news. Such a mess. We were planning on getting married. I had popped the question, and she'd accepted. We were looking at venues where we could hold an engagement party, were about to push the boat out for that and save up for a wedding over the next five years. What with Anna's father passing away, the last thing we wanted was for her mum to foot the bill… now she's… gone." A tear dripped onto his cheek, and his voice faltered. Embarrassed, he wiped his cheek with the sleeve of his overall. "Forgive me, I'm not usually the emotional type."

Sam swallowed down the lump lodged in her throat and said, "There's really nothing to forgive. You've had a hell of a shock, you're entitled to be emotional. Can I get you a glass of water?"

"No, I'm fine. I'll have a strong coffee in a mo. Unless I can get you a drink and we'll have one together?"

"We'll be up for that. Thanks, two white with one sugar, if you don't mind."

He hoisted himself off the desk and walked towards the door. He peered through the window overlooking the workshop and groaned. "I'll be right back. Shit, that's the boss coming in now."

"In that case, we'll come with you." Sam removed her ID from her pocket ready to show the boss who was rapidly approaching them.

"What's the meaning of this? Why were you in my office? I've told you before, McCoy, it's off limits to grease monkeys."

Sam was taken aback by the anger tearing through his tone. She raised her warrant card and nudged Bob to do the same. "DI Sam Cobbs and DS Bob Jones, and you are?"

"Umm... oh, I'm Fred Jackson. The police? What the heck are you doing here?"

"We were having a private conversation with one of your employees."

"There are other places you can do that. I pay him to work while he's here, not stand around gossiping with friends who are in the force."

Sam tutted. "We're not personal friends, we're here on official business. I think you're being totally unreasonable, Mr Jackson."

"In your opinion," he snapped.

Lee reappeared with three mugs of coffee.

"Oh great, now you're treating this place like a drop-in café as well."

"Give it a rest, boss. They've come to deliver some shocking news."

"What news? That the price of fuel is on the increase again...? Or that the cost of a joint of beef has gone through the roof? Newsflash, we're all aware we're going through a cost-of-living crisis."

Sam's blood seared her veins, and she stepped towards him. Bob tried to claw at her arm, but she shrugged him off.

"Now listen to me, Mr Jackson, I don't care for your tone. You're being totally asinine with your conception of what's going on here." She peered over her shoulder at Lee. "I'm going to have to tell him, if that's okay with you."

"Go for it, but he probably won't believe you."

"Believe what?" Jackson demanded.

Sam turned back to the irate boss and released an impatient sigh. "For your information, we've come here today to share the devastating news that what we believe to be Lee's girlfriend's body has been found." She let that sink in for a little while, keeping a close eye on Jackson's reaction.

His gaze flicked between Sam and Lee and over to Bob. A frown pulled at his already wrinkled brow. "Body? As in…?"

"Yes, that's right, she's dead, boss. Now, do you mind if I continue my conversation with the officers? Only I'm rather keen to assist them with their enquiries, if that's all right with you?"

"Jesus, man. What can I say? I feel foolish for being so petty. Go home, you shouldn't be here. The other guys can take over the job you're tackling at the moment."

Lee shook his head and stared down at the mug in his hand. "I'd rather stay at work and keep myself occupied. If I go home, memories of Anna will be all around me… I can't deal with that, not right now."

"Very well. Go back in my office then. I'm sorry to have disturbed you."

Sam believed Jackson's words to be genuine enough, and her temper shrank along with his change of attitude.

Jackson bowed his head and walked through the workshop back out to his car.

"That'll teach him to think before he speaks next time," Sam muttered, her gaze still fixed on Jackson.

"It won't," Lee assured her. "He spends most of his life flying off the handle about one thing or another. As his employees, we usually take the brunt of his frustrations."

"He needs to take a chill pill in that case. It's not right, talking to his members of staff like that," Sam replied.

"We're used to it. I knew I'd get into bother using his office. You wait, he'll hit the roof again once he lays eyes on the marks on his desk left by my greasy overalls." Lee chuckled. His face straightened almost immediately. "Where were we?"

Sam raised her mug. "About to have a drink. Let's do that first and then get back to it."

"Suits me. First break I've had this morning."

"What about the other two men, don't they pull their weight around here?" Sam asked. She cast a glance over her shoulder at his colleagues, still nattering over a sandwich and a drink, her own break forgotten about.

"They have their moments. It's quite quiet around here at the minute. I let them get on with it, can't be arsed standing around doing sod all, hate it when the time drags. I do my work and get home… I used to have a life. I suppose all that's going to change now that Anna is no longer with us." He took a sip of his drink and walked back into the office.

"This is going to be tough on him. I think it's starting to hit him now," Bob muttered beside her.

Sam took a sip from her cup and said, "Yep, I think dealing with his boss is about to open up the floodgates. You up for this?"

"Do I have a choice?"

"Nope."

They joined Lee in the office, and Bob closed the door behind him.

"We need to ask some really nitty-gritty questions about your relationship with Anna, are you up to it?" Sam asked.

"I guess we'll see, won't we? What do you need to know?"

"Has Anna hinted at any personal problems lately, maybe at work?"

"No, she was well liked by all of her colleagues. She was a dental nurse, not sure if you knew that or not."

"We didn't. Where did she work?"

"At a private clinic on the outskirts of Workington. Drakes is the name."

Bob removed his notebook and pen from his pocket.

"Has she had any cause to be concerned with regard to anyone following her recently?"

He paused to think and then shook his head. "I can't think of anything. Do you think someone was…? What do they call it? Stalking her, that's it, isn't it?"

"Perhaps, but then, if she hadn't mentioned anything to you about it, I suspect we're way off the mark. What about clients? Was there ever an issue there?"

"In what respect?"

"Any confrontations we should be aware of?"

Again, he took another pause to reflect. "Not to my knowledge. She wasn't the type to have confrontations with people."

"Did you argue as a couple?"

"No, never. Maybe little squabbles about me leaving the loo seat up or the top off the toothpaste, but in the main, no, she was pretty easy-going."

"What about hobbies? Did you have separate hobbies?"

"I like to tinker on my mates' cars at the weekend. I'm eyeing up a kit car to build, but that's not in my immediate future. We have, sorry, had, a wedding to save for."

Sam felt the need to reach out and touch his arm. She didn't. "I'm sorry, not much longer."

"It's okay. I'm dealing with it. I'm desperate to help you,

so please, don't stop if you think the questions are doing some good."

"They are, if only to discount certain issues. I'll go as quickly as I can. Did Anna have any hobbies, apart from swimming in the lakes?"

"Not really. That and going out with the girls a couple of times a week."

"Did she usually swim in the same area or travel around?"

"There was a group of them who belonged to the same club. They used to meet up regularly and swim at different locations. She always told me that she felt alive when she was wild swimming."

"And the club she attended, is that in Buttermere?"

"It's on the outskirts."

"Any idea what it's called?"

"I'll have to think about that one. It's Brave something."

Bob removed his phone from his pocket and came up with a lead. "Brave Endeavours?"

"Sounds about right. Sorry, I'm hopeless with names of clubs and that sort of thing."

"We'll visit them, see what we can find out," Sam said. "We can't thank you enough for speaking to us, you've been a tremendous help."

"I might think of something else once you've gone. Do you want to leave me your number, just in case?"

Sam handed him one of her business cards. "I was about to suggest the same. Call me anytime, day or night. Sometimes important details can come to you when you least expect them to."

"I'll try not to disturb you at night, I know I wouldn't like it. I hope you get what you're looking for at the club. I'm sure they'll tell you the same, that Anna was devoted to swimming."

"It was nice meeting you. You have our assurance that

we'll do our very best to get you the justice you and Anna deserve."

"I hope so. I'm going to miss her terribly, still can't believe she's gone. It's awful to think your life can be disrupted at the click of the fingers or blink of an eye."

"Hopefully, we'll have the answers for you soon."

"I hope so. I'll show you out. The boss is probably eager to get back into his office."

"If he gives you any bother, send him in my direction and I'll sort him out for you."

Lee smiled at the prospect. "I'll do that. Thanks for taking on the case, Inspector. I have a good feeling about you and your partner dealing with the investigation."

"We rarely let anyone down, you have my word on that, Lee. Take care. I'll be in touch again soon. Good luck telling Anna's mother."

"Crap, I forgot all about that. I'll ask the boss if I can grab an hour for lunch and nip over there now."

Mr Jackson saw them coming and exited his car. He passed Sam and Bob and said nothing on his way into the workshop.

"Bloody twat," Bob whispered.

Sam laughed. "Couldn't have put it better myself. Have you got the address for the club?"

Bob held his phone up. "I have. Want me to punch it in?"

Her eyebrows raised. "Obviously."

En route to the club, Sam received a call from Des. "Hi, have you got something for me?"

"I'm in the middle of doing the PM on Anna Ritter, and I believe I have some valuable information for you."

"Which is?"

"Once I stripped off her clothing, it was evident that she had been physically attacked. She had fingermark bruising around her wrists and at the tops of her legs. Further examinations to the vagina revealed that she had sexual intercourse a few hours before her death."

"Intercourse, or are you telling me she was raped?"

"I would speculate it was the latter. I've taken swabs. I won't know the results for a few days, if there are any to be had, given that she was found in the lake."

"Bugger, yes, I never thought about that, that'll teach me to get my hopes up about any possible DNA. Do your best for me."

"Don't I always? Anyway, I must plod on, just thought you should be made aware of that piece of information."

"Thanks, I appreciate it, Des. Ring me if anything else crops up. We've spoken to the boyfriend. He's told us that Anna was an expert swimmer and belonged to a wild swimming club. We're on our way to have a word with them now."

"Okay, that sounds promising. Do you know if the two victims knew each other?"

"The boyfriend didn't recognise Fern's name when I asked the question."

"Hmm... maybe you'll get more from the club. Gotta fly. Speak later." With that, he ended the call.

"He's an odd bugger," Bob stated, his tone flat.

"Yeah, in all fairness, I've yet to meet a pathologist who isn't." Her mobile rang again, and she answered the call without seeing who it was, thinking it would be Des again. "Hi, did you forget to tell me something?"

"Sam, it's me, Chris."

Sam glanced sideways to see Bob clench his fist. "What do you want, Chris? I've told you time and time again that your solicitor needs to go through my solicitor, that should be the end of the matter."

"It's not as easy as that. Sam, I need to see you, it's urgent. I don't know where to turn for help."

Bob leaned forward so she could see him while she

focused on the road ahead. He sliced his finger across his throat, telling her to cut the call, but she picked up on the desperation that was unmistakeable in Chris's tone.

"Go on, surprise me. What is it you're after?"

"You."

"What?" She shot a glance at Bob whose mouth had dropped wide open. "What are you talking about?"

"I want you back. I know you're still in love with me, you're not the type to fling everything in the air and say it doesn't matter. You love me as much as I love you, always have and always will."

"You're deluded if you believe that, Chris. All this is about you losing out on the house, isn't it?"

"No, I don't care about the money. All I want is another chance with the woman I love."

Bob mumbled something indecipherable.

"What was that? Who was it? Shit, have you got me on speaker?"

"I thought you were the pathologist calling me back about the investigation I'm handling at present. Bob's in the car with me."

"Hi, Chris," Bob said and stuck two fingers up.

"Bob. How's things?" It was a question that came across as anything but heartfelt.

"Like you care, mate. Get a life and leave the boss alone, or you'll have me to deal with, you hear me?"

The line went dead.

Sam thumped Bob's thigh. Livid, she demanded, "What gives you the right to interfere in a conversation that doesn't concern you?"

"Well, he had it coming. How long has he been pestering you? He needs to get a grip, stop making a fool of himself."

"Yeah, and I should be the one to tell him to get on his

sodding bike, not you, got that? I had the situation under control until you stuck your damn nose in."

"Pardon me for caring about a friend."

"There's a difference between caring and trying to run someone's life for them."

Bob growled and hit the dashboard with his clenched fist.

"Were you wishing that was my head?" Sam queried.

"Don't be so absurd. I'm frustrated. All I was doing was sticking up for a friend."

"You weren't. What you were doing was meddling in my relationship."

"What? You no longer have a relationship, or have you forgotten?"

"Of course I bloody haven't. Stop nit-picking and winding me up, Bob."

"If this was Rhys sitting here, how would he have reacted?"

"I suspect with more decorum than you have in your little finger."

"Charming, that is. Forget it, I wish I hadn't bothered now."

Sam sighed and slapped the steering wheel. "That makes two of us. I'm going to call him back and I want you to keep quiet, understand?"

Bob folded his arms and turned to look out of the side window.

"I said, do you understand?"

"Yes, boss. I'll tell you what, why don't you pull over and let me out of the damn car while you speak to that dickhead?"

"Suits me." Sam indicated and drew into a parking space. Her partner leapt out of the car, slammed the door and proceeded to pace the pavement.

She redialled Chris's number. It rang and rang and then

clicked into voicemail. She refused to leave a message, preferring to speak to him in person. She lowered the passenger window and tooted her horn. "Get in, Bob."

Her partner entered the car. They stared at each other for a few uncomfortable moments, and then Sam pressed down on the accelerator and the car shot off before Bob had attached his seatbelt.

"I'm sorry," she mumbled.

"Me, too," he replied, if a little reluctantly.

"You shouldn't have done it," she added quickly, not quite willing to move on.

"I think we've established that already. Can we forgive and forget?"

"Done. I know you were only watching out for me, but I'm a grown woman, Bob. I don't need to be supervised."

"Really?" he asked then laughed.

Sam joined in. "Maybe sometimes."

"You've got that right."

CHAPTER 7

When they arrived at the club, they found the doors locked.

"Shit, I knew we should have called ahead," Bob complained.

"Why didn't you then? Instead of sitting there, twiddling your thumbs."

"Ouch, that was uncalled for."

"Ignore me. Wait, there's a car drawing up behind us, maybe all is not lost after all."

A slim woman in her fifties locked up the VW Beetle and walked towards them. "Hi, can I help you?"

Sam and Bob produced their warrant cards.

"DI Sam Cobbs, and my partner, DS Bob Jones. Are you the owner or manager of the club?"

"Yes, I have been for the past ten years or more. What brings the police to my door? Have I broken the law?" Her brow knitted with concern, she inserted the key into the lock and looked at the darkening sky overhead. "You'd better come in unless you want to chance getting soaked."

"Good idea. Sorry, I didn't get your name?"

"How remiss of me, I didn't offer it. I'm Brenda Cavendish."

"Thank you for allowing us in, Mrs Cavendish."

"I hope I don't live to regret it. Come through to my office. I need to switch on a few lights first, and the heating. Brr… it's cold in here today. Winter has arrived, unfortunately."

"In full swing, I'd say, after the downpours we've experienced this past week or so."

They ventured into a small office where Brenda flicked on an oil heater beside her desk. "Have a seat, what's this all about?"

"It's not pleasant, just to warn you."

"Oh dear, whatever can you mean?"

They all took a seat. Bob removed his notebook in readiness, and Sam inhaled a deep breath in preparation.

"Unfortunately, we're dealing with a murder investigation. Actually, two separate ones, but we believe both crimes may be linked."

"Murder? Dear oh dear. But what does this have to do with the club?"

"We believe one of the victims was a member here. Anna Ritter."

"Oh no. How utterly dreadful." Brenda covered her eyes with one of her hands. "That's such terrible news. She was such a lovely lady." Her hand dropped to reveal watery eyes. "May I ask how she died? Please, don't go into detail if it's too gory."

"Sadly, she drowned."

"No way. Well, that has totally shocked me. She was one of the strongest swimmers at this club. I can't believe what you're telling me."

"It's true. What we suspect to be her body was found in Buttermere Lake very early this morning."

"Goodness me, but she always went swimming early. Are you telling me she got into some kind of difficulty?"

"Possibly, but very unlikely. A post-mortem is being performed at the moment. We'll know more as to the cause of death once the pathologist files his report."

Brenda placed her hand on top of the radiator and shivered. "I can't believe it. She would never drown. Out of all the people who attend this school, she would be the one I would least expect to get into difficulty."

"I'm sorry, no, you've misunderstood me. We believe it was intentional as she was murdered."

"Oh gosh, how silly of me, you did say that, didn't you?"

"It's the shock. I have to ask, do you also know Fern Mitchell?"

Her head was dipping up and down before Sam had uttered the surname. "I do. She went missing last week, and her body… oh no, I heard on the news that she had also been murdered."

"How did you know Fern?"

"She was also a member of this club."

"Okay. And they were both strong swimmers?" *Not that it mattered a jot in Fern's case, especially as she was shot.*

"Oh yes, the pair of them would often have races in the lakes at the end of a session. Some might perceive it as showing off, but I never saw it that way. It was beautiful to watch, they were graceful and so skilful in the water. A marvellous sight to behold, I can tell you. What a tragedy this is, to lose them both within a few days of each other."

"I know, it's hard to take in. What we need to ascertain is whether these two women had any problems while they were here."

"What type of problems?"

"Did they ever fall out with any of the other members?"

"No. For one thing, I wouldn't stand for any of that

nonsense. I run a good club, a place where members can come and have fun. Everyone got along well together, mostly. I suppose there has been the odd spat over the years but nothing too detrimental. It was all sorted out with a firm handshake over a nice cup of tea."

"Very civilised."

"Yes, that's the word I was searching for. But that was between a couple of male members."

"Male members? Oh, I presumed it was an all-women's club."

"Oh, no. The men make up about a third of our membership."

"Their age ranges?"

"Between eighteen and seventy-seven, I believe. That's off the top of my head."

"I see. And how many members do you have in total?"

"Let me think, at the last count, which was a few months ago, it stood at eighty-six."

"And they attend the club every week, or every month?"

"Whenever they like, there's no pressure from me, within reason. What I will say is, we always have a good turnout."

"When was the last time you met up as a group?"

"That would have been last Friday. We heard that Fern was missing and we all wanted to help out with the search. Our intentions were good, but we didn't know where to start looking first. Wayne gave us some pointers as to where she went missing and what her daily routine was like. We hunted around for a couple of hours, but I felt we were in the way most of the time."

"It was kind of you to help out, you didn't have to. How many of the group showed up to lend a hand?"

"The majority of them. A couple were away on either business meetings or had family issues to deal with, and one member had just lost his mother to cancer and had her funeral to arrange, otherwise he would have joined us. They all wanted to do the right thing. They gave up their spare time without any complaints. The only downside was that our search proved to be pointless."

"At least you did your best and tried to lend a hand, where many people wouldn't have bothered."

"That's because we care about each other."

"Always nice to hear. I don't suppose we could have a list of the members and possibly their contact details, could we?"

"I don't see why not. For any specific reason?"

"Just keeping everything in order. I'd rather gather all the details as we go along than have to revisit something vital at a later date."

"Let me organise that for you now. A few of the members are due to join me for a small gathering in about half an hour for a strategy meeting."

Sam inclined her head. "A strategy meeting? What does that entail?"

"It's just a grand name for a few of us putting our heads together to plan the swims we intend to carry out over the next few months."

"How many are coming?"

"Four more people. The others trust us to make the right decisions for everyone. It's worked out well so far."

"What about Fern and Anna, would they have been part of the strategy meetings in the past?"

"No, they were far too busy to spare the time to join us. Like me, these people are slightly older, that's me putting it politely." She smiled and then sighed. "It's very sad to think that neither Fern nor Anna will ever join us on a swim again. Very sad indeed." Tears glistened in her eyes. "I'm sorry, I'm not usually the type to break down in front of strangers, but there again, I've never had to deal with two friends being murdered before either."

"Please don't apologise, it's natural to feel the way you do being given such unexpected news. Would it be possible to hang around and speak to the others?"

"Of course. I hope they can be of help to your investigation. Let me sort out a copy of the list you need. Can I get you a drink while you wait?"

Sam raised a hand. "We're good, thank you. We've not long had one at a previous visit."

Brenda left her desk and crossed the room to the four-drawer file cabinet in the corner. She unlocked it with a key from the bunch she was holding and ran her fingers across the files until she reached the one she was after. She withdrew it and retook her seat behind the desk. "What do we have here then?" She studied the list and nodded. "Yes, this is the most up to date one."

Sam picked up on that. "Up to date? Meaning there are others? Are you telling me that some members have left the club?"

"Every club has to deal with the same issue, I believe. One's circumstances change. A few of our members have moved out of the area in the past few months. They wanted to remain on the books, but the practicalities simply didn't add up, so between us, after much deliberation, we decided it would be better for them to give up their membership and join a club in their new area."

"Do members have to pay a yearly fee here?" Sam asked.

"Yes, it's only fifty-five pounds a year. That covers the admin costs and sometimes the need to hire a coach now and again."

"I see."

Brenda sorted through the paperwork in the file and then glanced over her shoulder. "I suppose I'd better see if the printer is working, it can be very temperamental at times. I dread using it most days. They really can be more trouble than they're worth." She left her seat and switched the machine on. It churned as it warmed up. The noise died down once it was ready. Brenda lifted the lid and pressed the button. She switched the machine off again and returned to her seat. She slid the sheet of paper across the desk to Sam.

Sam surveyed the list, noted all the addresses were within a twenty-five- to thirty-mile radius of where they were now. "Some of them come quite a way then?"

"Yes, they're committed, that's for sure. Once the adrenaline for wild swimming hits you, I'm afraid it's very difficult to get out of your system. The members who are farther afield at one time lived in the immediate area and insisted they remain members. Which is always fine by me. It was different with the others who chose to move to a different county, many miles away. We have a lovely group of people here, sadly missing two very strong members now that Fern and Anna are both gone. Two exceptional swimmers. It doesn't make sense that they should lose their lives involved in something they enjoyed doing in their spare time. It doesn't make sense at all to me. Nope, not one iota."

"Can you tell me if anyone ever fell out with the two victims?"

Brenda frowned and shook her head. "No, I can't see it. They were genuinely nice ladies with a passion for this club and for swimming, that's why I'm struggling to comprehend they're both dead."

Sam could tell the woman was getting herself in a tizzy. "It's fine. Sorry, I had to ask the question."

"I don't blame you for asking either. It's the emotion welling up inside, it's catching me out now and again. You'll have to forgive me for getting myself into such a state. You see, all the members are like an extended family to me. Since my husband passed away, I've thrown myself into doing what's right for the club and its members. I'm rarely at home these days. There are far too memories to battle in the house, it's become a very maudlin place to live in."

"That's very sad. I'm sorry for your loss and how it has affected you. Have you thought about moving?"

"Yes, a couple of the ladies here sat me down last month and gave me a good talking-to, assured me that I would be doing the right thing if I put the house up for sale and moved on. Dave will always live here, in my heart, but being in that house..." She shuddered. "It gives me the creeps."

"Hopefully you'll find a buyer soon. I wish you luck in that department."

A car door sounded outside. "That's very much appreciated, thank you. Ah, sounds like someone has arrived. I'll need to open the door and let them in. I won't be long."

"Take your time, we're in no rush."

Brenda left the room.

"In no rush?" Bob queried.

"Shut up, Bob. Not every part of an investigation needs to take place at warp speed, you know."

"If you say so. It's just that we're not getting very far here, and it's driving me loopy."

"You need to learn to be more patient, partner. It can stand you in good stead during cases such as this."

"If you say so," Bob mumbled.

The door opened, and in breezed Brenda once more. "It was two of our older members. I broke the news to them. Wish I hadn't now."

"Is there something wrong?"

"Nothing physically wrong with them, but their emotions are taking a battering. I mentioned you might need a chat with them. Did I do the right thing?"

"Yes. Shall we speak with them now?"

Brenda nodded. "Why not? It's not like I can tell you anything else. Come this way, I'll introduce you."

The three of them left the office and entered the large function room, yet unseen by either Sam or Bob.

"This is where we hold all of our meetings," Brenda said. "There are a couple of toilets at the back and a small kitchen area. We like to put on a little spread at the end of each meeting, something else the membership covers—occasionally but not all the time. A lot of the members bring a plate of food in from home with the intention of sharing it with the others. Anyway, you don't need to know the ins and outs of what we get up to around here. I'll introduce you to the others. They must be in the kitchen, fixing themselves a cup of tea. Are you sure you don't want a drink?"

Bob gave a slight cough beside Sam. "Go on then, you've twisted our arms. Two white coffees with one sugar, thank you," Sam said.

"Why don't you assemble a few chairs, there's a pile in the corner there, and I'll make the drinks?"

Bob set off in the opposite direction and collected five chairs which he placed in a circle in the centre of the room. Sam shuffled her feet until the three members of the club joined them. Brenda handed Sam and Bob their drinks, and all of them sat.

"This is Jim Baker and Tina Albright. I'm sorry, I can't remember your names?"

Sam smiled. "I'm DI Sam Cobbs, and this is DS Bob Jones. We're sorry to show up like this, but I'm sure you'll forgive us in the circumstances."

"Shocking news. Wasn't expecting to hear anything like that today," Tina replied.

"Did you know the two ladies well?" Sam asked the woman who was in her late sixties to early seventies. She had snowy-white curly hair and slim features.

"As well as anyone else, I suppose. They were fine women

who loved nothing better than being out there, in the cold water. Do you swim?"

Sam shrugged. "In all honesty, I prefer to swim in warm water. I'd freeze to death if I ventured into one of the lakes. Even for a paddle, they're super cold, aren't they?"

The three members all nodded.

"It takes some getting used to, granted," Jim said. "But it's invigorating once you get used to it. You feel so alive, your body tingles all over."

"I saw a lady on the local news talking about it a few months ago, she said pretty much the same thing. I wouldn't say that swimming has ever really been at the top of my to-do list in this life. I do, however, enjoy a bit of hill-walking now and again."

"Ah yes, it's either one or the other around here, isn't it?" Brenda added.

"Maybe I should take it up, after hearing about these two tragedies," Jim muttered.

Brenda and Tina both nodded.

"Please, don't let these two incidents put you off doing what you love," Sam said. "It would be a shame if you threw in the towel now… ouch, no pun intended."

Bob groaned beside her.

"Do you know why the women died?" Jim asked. "Sorry to come right out and ask the obvious. My father used to be a local bobby in the area. Let's just say I have an inquisitive mind."

Sam smiled and said, "I understand. No, we have very little to go on for now. The investigation into Anna's murder only began this morning, once her body had been discovered in the lake, and I have to say, unfortunately, we haven't made much progress since Fern's body was found on Wednesday. All we can surmise at present is that both women had been held captive somewhere before they were killed."

"Both of them were reported missing. Are you saying that they had likely been abducted?" Tina asked.

"That's the conclusion we've come to so far. It's likely that Anna was possibly abducted around the time Fern's body was dumped in the lake and she was shot."

"What?" Brenda asked, frowning. "Did it happen at the same place then?"

"Yes, at Derwentwater, that's where Anna's car was found by her boyfriend."

Jim sighed. "Is that where they both died?"

"No, strangely enough, Anna's body was found in Buttermere, first thing this morning."

"Why do you suspect someone killed them?" Jim asked. "If that's not a dumb question."

"It's not. The main clue leading us to that conclusion is that both women were found fully clothed. Also, in Fern's case, I'm not telling you what you haven't already heard on the news here, she was shot."

"A sniper shooting?" Jim shuffled to the edge of his seat.

"So it would seem. We're trying to figure out the timings. It's a possibility the killer was still around and maybe Anna was in the wrong place at the wrong time. Or the killer was aware of her routine. Of course, that's pure speculation on my part at this time. It would appear that Anna was abducted after her morning swim. However, I fear the true details won't come to light until we have a suspect in custody."

Jim puffed out his cheeks. "It's unimaginable that this sort of thing could happen in these parts. Do you think the person is local? Or might they be visiting the area? Come up here on a killing holiday... yeah, that was a ridiculous statement, maybe you should ignore that."

Sam lifted her shoulders and dropped them again. "It's something we need to consider. The investigation hasn't really got going yet. The early stages can be slow and laborious, but by interviewing people such as yourselves, we hope to gain more insight into the victims' characters and their movements over time."

"I wouldn't like your job for all the tea in China," Brenda said. "Please, ask any questions you need to ask. As a group, we'll see if we can answer them for you."

"I know you said they rarely fell out with anyone, but if you can try and cast your mind back, could either of the victims have had a confrontation with another member of the group?"

The three members all looked at each other, seemingly perplexed by the question.

"No, I can't think of anything," Brenda replied. "What about you, Jim and Tina?"

"Nope, nothing is coming to mind," Jim said. "We all get on so well here. I wouldn't belong to the club if I picked up on any kind of friction."

Tina nodded. "I'm of the same opinion. Life's too short to put up with crap like that. I've loved my time being a member. It's the highlight of my life, a great sense of camaraderie. Friends for life, that's how I perceive you all. Many of us are either divorced or widowed, aren't we, Brenda?"

"We are, dear. This club is a lifeline for a lot of people, but we also appreciate our other members who lead very full lives, too."

Sam asked a few more questions about the relationship between all the members and felt satisfied there wasn't anything irregular about either the club or its members. However, she would still get the team to thoroughly go through the list they'd been given, just to make sure.

"Okay, I think that's all we need to cover today. I can't thank you enough for speaking so openly with us," Sam announced.

She stood, and Bob followed suit.

"Thanks for the coffee," her partner said.

"I'll show you to the door." Brenda rose from her seat.

Tina and Jim both said goodbye.

"I hope you'll find the person responsible, soon. Just to clarify, do you believe there is any reason why we should fear for our safety?" Brenda asked.

"None whatsoever, although as a precaution, I do think that you and the rest of the members need to remain vigilant at all times."

"We'll be cautious. I will certainly emphasise the need to be, to our other members."

"Good, that's all we can ask. Take care."

"You, too." She closed the door and locked it on the inside.

CHAPTER 8

Sam's thoughts played havoc on the drive back to the station. "Why isn't this making any sense?"

"You know we get some cases that try us and push us to the limits. I get a sense that this is going to be one of those. All we can do is work with what we have in front of us. Talking of which, do you think it's worth us going through that list of names?"

They exited the car and made their way through the main entrance.

"We have to. We dismiss it at our peril. Every investigation demands us to be thorough, Bob."

"Yeah, I was just wondering if we would be wasting our time."

They climbed the stairs, and Sam glanced his way.

"Wasting our time? Even if we get a glimmer of hope from that list of names it could lead to bigger and better things. Why are you being such a negative Nigel about this?"

"I'm not. Well, maybe I am. I suppose I have a niggling feeling deep in my gut that I can't shift. I want to catch the killer as much as you do, but at what cost?"

"I'm not with you. Please explain your logic to me because I'm struggling to grasp it right now."

"I can't. I've tried to rid myself of the doubts, I guess you'd call them, but I haven't succeeded so far. Maybe it's too soon to get a real hold on the case."

"Perhaps. Don't be afraid to voice your concerns along the way, okay?"

"Yeah, will do. What are you going to do about Chris?"

"Damn, I'd forgotten all about him. That's how little he means to me now."

"Good, in that case, I'm sorry to have brought the subject up again."

"Don't be. I'll ring the solicitor, see what he can come up with."

"You're a wise lady. In my experience, it's always best to keep on top of these things. Don't let him think he's got one over on you, ever."

Sam smiled. "I try not to. I'm surrounded by good people, such as yourself, Bob."

Her partner swiped his hands together enthusiastically. "You only have to say the word and I'll go round there and give him a good seeing to and a piece of my mind."

"Really? Can you spare that much?"

Sam sniggered, and Bob stared at her, apparently perplexed enough for her to need to explain herself.

"A piece of your mind... can you spare that much...? Meaning... No, I'm not going there. It was a poor joke, one of many that has zoomed over your head in the last few months."

"What does that tell you?" he grumbled and pushed through the door to the incident room.

Sam wondered if he was tempted to let the door swing in her face as punishment for ticking him off. Thankfully, he didn't. Instead, he marched ahead of her, aiming for the drinks station. He glanced up and held a mug in the air. She gave him the thumbs-up and then proceeded to bring the whiteboard up to date.

Bob placed the coffee on the desk beside her and went back to his desk.

"Right, let me touch base with you all as to how our morning went. As you know, we were called out to Buttermere Lake this morning. We spoke to the witness who said he found the body behind a small island in the lake. The victim, Anna Ritter, was discovered fully clothed, just like the first victim. Her boyfriend reported her missing the same day Fern's body was found at Derwentwater."

"Hmm… so the killer took a chance and kidnapped her," Alex observed.

"Correct. At this point we weren't certain if the victims knew each other or not, but after speaking with…" Sam turned and circled the name she had written alongside the second victim, "her boyfriend, Lee McCoy, he informed us that Anna was an exceptional swimmer and even belonged to a wild swimming club."

"What about Fern?" Claire asked. "Did she belong to the club as well?"

Sam tapped the side of her nose. "Spot on, Claire. She did. After we had a chat with Lee McCoy, Bob and I zipped over to the club and spoke to the woman who runs it, Brenda Cavendish. She was understandably devastated to have lost two members within a few days of each other. Brenda also confirmed that both ladies were the best swimmers at the club."

"Very sad," Suzanna said.

"My sentiments exactly, Suzanna. Still, we mustn't dwell on this. If anything, knowing the truth should drive us on. I also received a call from the pathologist, informing me that during the PM, he found excessive bruising on Anna's wrists and the tops of her thighs, intimating that she had been sexually abused."

"Raped," Bob spouted.

"If you want to put it bluntly, yes, she'd been raped."

"What about DNA?" Claire asked. "Or would the water play a part in washing it away?"

Sam chewed her lip for a few seconds. "Des is hopeful that if any DNA has stuck, he'll come across it. That leaves us with what we obtained at the Brave Endeavours Swimming Club. Brenda gave us a list of all the members. What I need everyone to do is focus on the list, so I'm going to ask Claire to divide the names up between all of you. We need to ascertain whether any of the members have a record. I know it's a long shot, but it's really all we have at this moment."

"You believe someone inside the club is targeting the other members?" Alex asked, puzzled.

"Like I said, Alex, it's all we have right now, so we need to go with it. I'll leave that with you. Let me know what you find out. I have a few calls to make in my office." As if on cue, a phone rang in the distance. "They must have heard me. Good luck, folks." Sam trotted into her office. She grabbed the phone and said, "DI Sam Cobbs, how may I help you?"

"I… umm… don't hang up on me, Sam. I need to speak with you."

Sam closed her eyes, but the image of Chris walking out of her life entered her mind, and she forced them open again. "You've got two minutes, Chris, make them pay."

"What? I can't say what I want to say in that time."

"Make that one minute and forty-five seconds."

"You're being unreasonable, Sam. All I'm asking is that you allow me to say what I want to say without you putting unnecessary restrictions in my way."

"In case you hadn't noticed, I'm at work. You know how professional I am."

"That's what destroyed our marriage in the first place," he seethed.

"No, you dipping your wick elsewhere and walking out on me for over three weeks did that."

"Ouch, I deserved that."

"You did, because it happens to be the truth. Don't put the breakdown of our marriage on me, Chris. You hear me? All I ever did was work my socks off to make it work. I thought you had the same commitment, until I learnt that you had been having an affair. All those times I came home from work and you giving me the sob story of how hard you'd worked all day, dealing with customers before going back to the house to start on the renovations. You took me for a fool, no one does that."

"I didn't. Not really. These things happen in life, Sam. I regret what I did, that should be enough, shouldn't it?"

She glanced at her watch. "Sorry, your two minutes are up. I have an important investigation which needs my undivided attention. Have a nice life, Chris."

"Sam, don't you *dare* hang up on me."

Despite his warning, she did. Sam rounded her desk and flopped into the chair. Emotion overwhelmed her, and she slapped her hands over her face, doing all she could to suppress the tears threatening to fall.

"Knock, knock... can I come in? Hey, what's wrong?"

She glanced up to see Bob standing in the doorway with a cup of coffee in his hand.

"Is that for me?"

"It is, you forgot to pick it up. What's wrong, Sam?" He stepped inside the office and closed the door behind him.

She motioned for him to take a seat. He sat on the edge of the chair, his forearms on the desk.

"I'm feeling a little down, that's all."

His eyes narrowed. "You were okay before you came in

here to answer that call. Who was it? If anyone has upset you, they'll have me to deal with." He stared at her, his gaze burning into her soul. "It wasn't him again, was it?"

"It's okay, Bob. I dealt with him. Gave him two minutes, and when the time was up, I put the phone down."

"You may think you have the upper hand over him, but look at the state you're in. You're still allowing him to pull your strings, Sam."

"Say it as it is, partner. He's not. I want so much to wipe the floor with him every time I speak to him but I find myself holding back. This emotion is what I'm left with, a mixture of regret and stupidity on my part for ever believing we had a decent marriage to begin with."

"You must have had at one point."

She shook her head. "I can't recall any time he truly made me smile, unlike Rhys."

Bob grinned. "And there you have it. Why continue to live in the past when you have such a bright future ahead of you with such a brilliant guy?"

"I wouldn't say I'm guilty of living in the past. Maybe it's the regrets building up inside me. At the time, I thought we had a solid relationship. My fault, I had nothing really to compare it to. We'd been together since our teens. Any other dates I'd gone on before that usually fizzled out at the end of the first night. In the beginning, he did make me laugh. Perhaps I thought that's all it took to have a good relationship with a member of the opposite sex."

"Wrong, right? You know that now, don't you?"

"Indubitably."

Bob cringed. "There you go again with your fancy words."

Sam tipped her head back and laughed so hard her insides hurt. "Abigail doesn't know how lucky she is to have you."

"She would dispute that from time to time."

"Deep down you're a good man, Bob. Don't ever change, will you?"

"I'm sure if I did that, I'd have two feisty women breathing down my neck, one at home and the other one here, at work."

Sam smiled and nodded. "There's absolutely no doubt in my mind about that. Now go, let me get on with my work."

He stood and paused in the doorway. "Don't forget you were going to give your solicitor a call."

"I know. It's on my to-do list."

"My advice would be to get on to him now, while you're still worked up about things."

"I will. Go. Let's get things going on the investigation before the frustrations set in."

"I'm on the case, don't worry."

He left her to it, and Sam sucked in a few deep breaths to calm herself to a near normal level and then rang her solicitor. His secretary told her that he was on the phone and that she would get him to return her call once he was finished. Sam left it at that and set about tackling the post she'd neglected to deal with for a few days. The phone interrupted her a few minutes later. It was her solicitor, Mr Mayhew.

"Sam, how are you? You wanted a quick chat, I believe?"

"Hello, Mr Mayhew. Thanks for getting back to me so promptly. I wondered if you had any news for me."

"With regard to finalising the divorce, I take it?"

"Yes, only it seems to be dragging on a bit now, and Chris has started badgering me for money."

"He what? No, no, no, that should never happen. Right, leave things with me for a couple of days. I'll chase some people at my end, see if we can't get this all wrapped up ASAP. I must hold my hand up and admit that I'm guilty of taking my eye off the ball. It won't happen again."

"It's okay. I understand and appreciate how busy you are.

It's never easy juggling work when you're drowning in paperwork, I get that."

"You're too understanding at times. Never feel bad about picking up the phone and geeing things along. No one is perfect, we all make mistakes and slip up now and again."

"I agree. Thanks for the call. I'll leave it all in your capable hands then."

"You do that. We'll get it all done and dusted ASAP. In the meantime, I'll put a call in to his solicitor, ask him to advise his client to back off or suffer the consequences."

"Which are?"

"Ah, I'll need to consider those before I make the call." He laughed.

"I'll leave it with you."

"You do that, I won't let you down. You'll be a free woman again in a few days, guaranteed."

"That would be a dream come true. I'll speak to you soon."

"You will. Enjoy the rest of your day, Sam."

"You, too."

She ended the call and sat there, staring at the wall for a few seconds. *A free woman! It's been a long time coming. Something to look forward to.*

CHAPTER 9

"We've got some good news," Bob shouted from the doorway.

Sam's stomach clenched. She glanced up from the paperwork she'd been toiling over for the past few hours and removed her spectacles. "Don't keep me in suspense."

"Two of the members have previous convictions for assault, against women."

Sam flew out of her chair and followed him into the incident room. "Who? What kind of assault?"

"One rape, the other a stalking incident. Both men were put away for their crimes. Four years, and the other eighteen months."

"This could be the break we've been waiting for. Let's get them brought in for questioning. Liam, you and Suzanna pick up one of the suspects. Alex and Oliver, you grab the second one. Obviously, if they're not at home, which is likely to be the case during the day, unless they're on the dole, ask the neighbours where they work and, if necessary, pick them up from there. We'll do more background checks in your absence. Contact me as soon as you have them in the car and are on your way back. I'll interview them upon your return."

The four members of the team set off.

"What's wrong with your face?" Sam asked Bob.

"I thought we'd be the ones bringing them in," he whined.

"Get a grip, man. We can't do everything ourselves. Our expertise is needed here. So get cracking. Delve into their backgrounds. No, let me correct that..." She ran her finger down the list until she came to the two names which had been circled. "You take Robert Lang, Claire and I will take Joshua Hart."

His face morphed into dissatisfaction.

"Don't tell me you're going to complain about that not being fair now, aren't you?" Sam said.

His cheeks coloured up. "Me? Never! I wouldn't dream of it."

"We're wasting time. We need to get on with the task and be ready for when the team returns."

"On it."

Bob hurried back to his desk, and Sam pulled up a chair alongside Claire who was sniggering.

"Something wrong, Claire?"

"You have him wrapped around your little finger," Claire whispered with another chuckle.

Sam snorted. "If only that were true. He has his moments. Right, let's get to it. What do we know about Joshua Hart? Wait, before we start, did anything come back on the woman who went to Canada, Ivy's ex?"

"Sorry, I knew there was something I'd forgotten to tell you. Nope, nothing there. She's still out in Canada."

"Don't worry, it's been a hectic couple of days. Back to Hart, what have you got?"

"He's thirty, got put inside for rape back in twenty seventeen. No further incidents since then."

"Okay, so he would have come out three years ago with good behaviour. That's a positive sign if he hasn't had anything else pinned on him in the meantime."

"Might just mean that he's been lucky not to have been caught."

"Hmm… that's true. Let's look at the original crime he committed. What's the story there?"

"The victim was a former girlfriend. She claimed he showed up at her flat one night, drunk. Refused to leave. She threatened to call the police. He hit her, knocked her unconscious, and when she came round, he was on top of her."

"The bastard."

"He's always denied the charge, states that it never happened that way at all. Told the investigating officer that he called at the flat and she welcomed him in for a drink. They both had a few too many and ended up in bed together. The next day, she made up the cock-and-bull story because she felt ashamed. She shouted at him to get out. He went willingly. That evening, he felt confused when the police came knocking on his door to arrest him. He's protested his innocence ever since."

"Christ, that's a tough one. We've heard so many cases like this recently, it's getting hard to know who to believe."

"I agree. You're the best judge of character I've ever come across, boss, I'm sure you'll get to the bottom of what's right and wrong when you get to interview him."

"Thanks for the compliment. I doubt if it's true in some cases. My ex comes to mind."

Claire winced. "Sorry, I forgot about that. How's that going, or shouldn't I ask?"

"I've chased up my solicitor today, he's hoping to finalise the divorce in a few days. Chris is becoming a pain in the backside. He's already rung me more times than I care to mention today. I've had it up to here with him." She raised her flattened hand to just above her head. "He's even had the audacity to ask me to give him another chance."

Claire groaned. "Like that's going to happen. What's getting to him is the fact that you're all loved-up with another man."

Sam smirked. "Yep, I think you're right." She peered over her shoulder at Bob who was jotting down some notes. "How's it going over there?"

"It's going. You?"

"Yep, we're still digging."

"Sounds like it," he mumbled.

Sam faced Claire again and laughed. "He's still got a cob on with me."

"I haven't," he shouted.

"Whatever," Sam retorted then addressed Claire, "Have we got any information about what job he's doing now?"

Claire tapped the keyboard and brought up a screen. "Yes, according to his probation officer's report, he came out of prison and started working at a petrol forecourt."

"Is he still there?"

"Not sure. He was signed off after a year."

"With an exemplary record?"

"Yes. No further blemishes to his name."

"Okay. Let me contact Suzanna, see if they've picked him up yet."

She rushed for the phone just as it started ringing. "Hello, DI Sam Cobbs, can I help?"

"It's me, boss, Alex. We've picked up Lang, we're en route to the station now."

"Great job, see you soon, Alex." Sam raised her thumb at Bob. "Are you up to speed over there, or do you need Claire's expert advice to guide you?"

"Nope. All good. I'm all done and dusted here. What about you?"

"We're all finished. I'm going to call Suzanna now. We have a work address for the suspect that might be helpful to them." She placed the call. "Suzanna, it's me. How are you getting on?"

"We're on the way to his workplace now, a garage on the outskirts of Workington."

"Ah, you've got it. I was calling you to give you the details. We found the information on his probation sheet. Good luck. Let me know when you've picked him up, the others are on their way back to the station already."

"Will do, boss. We're almost there."

Sam ended the call and sat back. "I'll jot down some notes for the interview over another cup of coffee. Anyone else want one?"

"I never say no," Claire replied.

"Yep, me neither," Bob called across the room.

She fixed three coffees, and by the time she reached Claire's desk, another call had come in from Suzanna, letting her know that they had collected Hart and were on their way back.

Relieved that everything appeared to be going to plan, she took her coffee and returned to the office, calling over her shoulder, "Let me know when they arrive."

Twenty minutes later, Claire knocked on her door. "Wanted to let you know both suspects are waiting in the interview rooms for you, boss."

"Good. Thanks, Claire. I'll make my way down there now. Tell Bob to get ready to go, will you?"

"I will." Claire smiled and left the room.

Pad in hand, Sam walked out of her office and collected her partner on the way to Interview Room One. She found

Joshua Hart sitting at the table, his hands clenched tightly, looking uncomfortable in his surroundings.

"Thanks for coming in to see us, Mr Hart, we won't keep you too long."

"This is absurd. I've done nothing wrong," the suspect objected.

"Then you have nothing to worry about, do you?"

"What's this about anyway?"

"We'll get to that in a moment. I hope you have a good memory."

"What's that supposed to… oh, wait, has that bitch been spouting her mouth off again? I haven't been near her since I got out of prison, it was part of my probation terms."

"This isn't concerning your previous offence." She held up a hand to prevent any further objections. "Just hold fire a second while my partner begins the interview."

Bob switched on the recording machine and gave the relevant information to get the interview underway.

"Right, Mr Hart. May I call you Joshua or would you prefer Josh?"

"Josh will do. What's going on? One minute I'm at work, and the next you're hauling my arse in here and thrusting me into an interview room but have so far refused to tell me what this is all about."

"All is about to be revealed. I believe you're a member of the Brave Endeavours Swimming Club, is that correct?"

"Why are you asking when you already know the answer?"

"Is that correct?"

"Yes." He sighed and wrung his hands.

"How long have you been a member?"

"Since I came out. My probation officer advised me to take up a new sport, to ease me back into society. I like swimming, so decided I would challenge myself with wild swimming."

"And how has that worked out for you?"

"Very well up until now. The other members all get on great together. They accepted me, no questions asked."

"Do they know about your… background?"

"Brenda knows I was in prison, however, what I'd been in for never cropped up. You know I was innocent? Despite being found guilty."

"We only have your word for that, Josh."

"Yeah, and an ex-crim's word means fuck all, right?"

"There's no need for you to get irate."

"Seriously? How can you sit there and tell me that when you've dragged me in here for questioning? My boss was fucking livid. I bet he gives me the sack when I get back. He'll think up some excuse to get rid of me if he believes you lot are going to come down heavy on me all the time."

"We're not. All I need to ask you is a few questions about your whereabouts over the last ten days or so."

"Why?"

"We're investigating a couple of serious crimes during that time. That's all I'm prepared to say right now."

"Jesus, and I've come out at the top of your suspect list, is that it?"

Sam raised an eyebrow. "It's simple, tell us what we need to know and you can go back to work."

His chest inflated, and he let out a large sigh. "Which dates in particular?"

"Wednesday the fifth of October, where were you?"

"You're going to need to do better than that, Inspector. What time of the day are we talking about?"

"Specifically in the evening."

He paused to consider the question for a few moments and then snapped his finger and thumb together. "I was at a concert with a mate. Well, I say a concert, it was a local band playing at a venue in Workington."

"Does this mate have a name?"

"Mick Brookes. Do you want his number?"

"That would be helpful, yes."

He reached for his mobile, lying on the desk beside him and showed her the screen. She took the phone and passed it to Bob for him to jot down.

"And the venue?"

"Jesus, I'm not sure. The band was called The Skulls, a heavy metal band, they were okay, I suppose. Mick invited me along because his brother is one of the band members."

"I see. Okay, we'll check. I have another date for you. Early morning on Wednesday the twelfth of October, where were you then?"

"You're going to need to be more specific about the time."

"Let's say between six and eight a.m."

"Ah, right, okay, my shift starts at six-thirty every morning. So I was probably getting ready for work. I leave the house at around six-twenty. The petrol station is down the road from the flat I call home."

"And your boss can corroborate the time you show up for work?"

"Yeah, the camera clocks me in every day."

"Good, then all should be fine, providing you're telling us the truth, shouldn't it?"

He slammed his fist onto the table and glared at her. "I *am* telling the truth."

Sam cocked an eyebrow. "Really? And showing your temper in that way to the SIO on a double murder investigation isn't going to help your cause any."

His shoulders slumped. "Jesus, I didn't mean anything by it. Put yourself in my position. I was thrown into prison for something I didn't do, and now, every time something like this rears its head in the media, I'm pounced on and brought in for questioning. How is that right?"

Sam tilted her head and asked, "Are you telling me that you've been brought in for questioning before this?"

"No, I'm not saying that. This is the first time, but I can now see it becoming the norm, happening more and more in the future because you've just put me on the radar. Tell me I'm wrong."

Sam wagged her finger. "Wrong. The only reason you're here today is because you're a member of the same club the victims belonged to."

He held her gaze. "So if I were to hang around long enough I would see all the other members of the club being accompanied to the station to be interviewed, would I?"

Shifting uncomfortably, she replied, "No. You and one other."

"There's another member with a criminal record, is that it?"

"Yes. That's right."

"I take it that record was for crimes against a woman or women."

"Affirmative."

"I rest my case." He growled. "There are over seventy, possibly eighty members at that club, and you're only dragging two of us in for questioning. Does that seem fair to you?"

"When you put it that way, I suppose it doesn't, no. But if you look at things from my perspective, it would be remiss of me not to 'jump on the obvious', wouldn't it?"

He ran a hand over his face. "You still don't get it, do you? I was thrown into prison an innocent man and I'm going to spend the rest of my life being persecuted by the police, all because one woman chose to make up lies about me in an act of revenge. How is that justified?"

"It's not, if that's what truly happened."

Josh slammed his fist down again. "It is. I demand to speak to your senior officer because I'm clearly getting nowhere fast with you. I have rights, to be treated like a human being, I'm aware of that, and yet, here I am, being forced to give you an alibi for my whereabouts on two separate dates."

"I'm sorry you feel that way. You won't be allowed to meet with my senior officer, he's a very busy man. If, however, you have a problem with the way I've treated you today, then feel free to lodge a complaint. You'll find the address on our website."

His head dropped, and he stared at his clenched hands. "Like it would be worth it. The police close ranks, and there's no getting through the barriers you guys put up. How many times do we hear in the news that the Complaints Federation has upheld a complaint against the police? Never, or very rarely, that's how many."

"It does happen. I'm not trying to badger you. This interview is part of the process, I can assure you. All I'm seeking to do is find out who murdered these two women. If that means ticking you off or anyone else at the club, then..." Sam shrugged, "I'm sorry."

He glanced up at her, his gaze locked on hers. "You haven't told me who the women are."

"Fern Mitchell and Anna Ritter."

He shook his head. "Never. Bloody hell."

"You knew them?"

"Silly question. They were 'the megastars' of our club. The best swimmers, the ones we all strive to become one day. Obviously, you don't know who killed them, otherwise I wouldn't be here. Do you know why? Or how?"

"They both died in the water. One was shot and the other drowned."

"Fuck. Drowned? There's no bloody way that would happen to either one of them, they were both exceptional swimmers. I'm… well, it's not often I'm lost for words, like I am right now."

"Did you have any other connection with the two women?"

"No, nothing. I admired them from afar… not like that, admired their swimming abilities. Once they got in the water, nothing else mattered. They were as much at home in the lakes as on dry land. Never complained about the coldness of the water, the weather, nothing. It was a sheer pleasure for them both to be out there, swimming. The rest of us sometimes stood on the shoreline in awe, simply watching them glide through the water. It was a mesmerising sight, I can assure you. Damn, I can't believe they're both gone. May they both rest in peace."

"When was the last time you saw them?"

"I haven't been to the club for about two to three weeks, due to working extra hours to try and cover the bills. I've missed not attending. I find it a great release."

"The last time you met up, did you see anything suspicious, either with other members or possibly any strangers hanging around the club or at the location where you swam that day?"

"No, nothing is coming to mind at all. Sorry, if I could help, I would."

"Okay, this interview is now terminated. Thank you for coming in and helping us with our enquiries today. We'll check into the alibis you've given us. You're free to go. Do you need a lift back to work?"

"That would be great. And I apologise for losing my temper, I shouldn't have done that. I never used to be an angry man, but certain life events change your personality traits for the worst sometimes."

"I understand, and your apology is accepted. Thank you for sparing us the time to have this little chat today." Sam smiled and left her seat.

The PC standing at the back of the room came forward and tapped Hart on the shoulder. He pointed at the door. "I'll show you out."

Sam watched them walk down the hallway and breathed out a sigh. "One down, one to go."

"You believe him?" Bob asked.

The two men turned the corner out of view at the bottom of the hallway.

Sam faced her partner and nodded. "Actually, I do. One hundred percent. Don't you?"

Bob waved his hand from side to side. "The jury, as they say, is still out for me."

"On to the next one. Hopefully, Mr Lang will supply us with information that will give the investigation some momentum."

"I wouldn't hold my breath if I were you."

Sam tutted and entered the second interview room. A man in his early forties was sitting at the table. A female PC was watching over him from her post at the back of the room. Sam acknowledged the PC with a slight smile and made her way to the table. She sat opposite Robert Lang, and Bob said the necessary verbiage for the recording to start the interview.

"Why am I here? I've done my time. It's not right that you should hound me like this. Do I need a solicitor?"

"First of all, we've brought you in to help us with our enquiries."

"So I heard. What they didn't tell me was, regarding what."

"Two serious crimes that have been committed in the last week or so."

"Right, and what have they got to do with me? No, wait, there's no need for you to tell me, this is to do with my criminal record, isn't it?"

Sam nodded. "Not only that but because you're a member of the Brave Endeavours Swimming Club."

He frowned. "Yeah, along with what, seventy to eighty other people? Why pick on me just because I've got a record?"

"All we need to know is where you were on two specific dates. The first is the fifth of October, early morning."

"Probably in bed. Although I can't be certain."

"Where do you work, Mr Lang?"

"At the local bowling alley. My shifts generally take place from eleven in the morning to around midnight. I tend to sleep in until about nine, maybe ten the next day. Does that help you?"

"Are you single?"

"No, I have a girlfriend."

"Can she vouch for you?"

"For the fifth?"

"Yes."

"I suppose so. We spend most days at my gaff."

"And what about the twelfth?"

"What about it?" He frowned.

"Where were you early on that day, before nine?"

"Same thing, probably tucked up in bed. Are you going to tell me what crimes have been committed?"

"Two murders."

He blew out a breath. "How does having a stalking conviction turn me into a blasted murderer? That is what you're saying, isn't it?"

"No, all we're trying to determine is where certain people, who were known to the victims, were at the time of their deaths."

"Known to the victims? Who are they?"

"Fern Mitchell and Anna Ritter."

The colour in his cheeks drained. "What the actual fuck! Both dead, is that what you're telling me? How is that even possible? They were... Jeez, really lovely ladies."

"That's what we're trying to find out. Did you have much to do with either of them?"

"I knew Fern far better than Anna. Fern was a sweetheart, nothing was ever too much trouble for her. Always watching people swim, handing out tips on how to perform better. People listened to her because she was the best. She was willing to spend an extra five minutes discussing others' failures in the water, eager for them to improve. One in a million in my eyes. She taught me a lot in the few years I've known her. I can't believe she's no longer with us. Both dead... that's going to be so destructive for the group."

Sam frowned. "May I ask why?"

"Those two in particular always supported everyone else's attempts to do better in the water. Both of them now gone, why? It's so hard to fathom."

"Which is why we're interviewing people from the club."

"Ah, I get it now. It's reassuring to know this has nothing to do with my past record."

Sam squirmed in her seat. "It hasn't. Have you ever seen any suspicious activity at the club surrounding either of the women?"

He paused for a while and then shook his head. "No, nothing that I can think of. Such as?"

"A stranger hanging around at any of the locations you've visited recently."

"Nothing is coming to mind, sorry. You think someone was following them? Or possibly stalking them?"

"There's a possibility. If you let my partner have your girlfriend's phone number, we'll give her a call to corroborate your alibi."

"Is that it? You've made a big song and dance about this and are now setting me free without asking me in-depth questions?"

"What questions would you prefer me to ask you instead?"

Bob slid his notebook across the table. "Write her number down."

Lang removed his phone from his pocket to look up his girlfriend's number and jotted it in the notebook, which he then pushed back to Bob. "I don't know, do I, you're the coppers on a mission. I had nothing to do with their murders. They were really lovely women, helpful and just plain nice people to be around. I'm a reformed character, in case you're wondering."

"I can tell. We appreciate you coming in and speaking with us. You're free to go once we've spoken to your girlfriend. What's her name?"

"Molly. She's a bit younger than me, try not to scare her."

"Don't worry, I won't. We'll be right back." Outside the room, Sam dialled the number. "Hello, is this Molly?"

"It is, who wants to know?" the young woman demanded, a wary edge to her tone.

"My name is DI Sam Cobbs of the Cumbria Constabulary."

"Oh my, is something wrong?"

"No, it's nothing like that. We're investigating a couple of serious crimes in the area and questioning a few people who knew the victims. Your name has been put forward as an alibi by someone we've just questioned."

"What are you talking about? I don't understand."

"Robert Lang kindly agreed to come in to help us with our enquiries, and he's told us he was with you on the fifth of

October. That's Wednesday of last week, first thing in the morning. Can you confirm that?"

"What? He's been arrested?"

"No, that's not the case at all. He's genuinely helping us with our enquiries."

"Bugger off! Just because I'm young it doesn't mean I'm bloody stupid. What's he supposed to have done? And yes, I know he was inside. He promised me he'd changed, and now he's there, sitting in the cop shop, under suspicion."

Sam leant against the wall and tipped her head back. *Give me bloody strength. Why do people fly off the handle all the time?* "I think you must have got the wrong end of the stick. Robert hasn't been arrested for anything, I said he was helping us with our enquiries. Can you tell me if he was with you on Wednesday the fifth of October, between six and nine in the morning?"

"Yes, I think so. You know what? I can do without all this shit. I've never been contacted by the police before and never want to again. Tell him from me he's fucking dumped."

"No, wait. You're taking this too far. Molly? Molly?" Sam stared at the phone and then pushed away from the wall. "Shit, she hung up on me... after she sodding well dumped him. How the heck am I going to tell him?"

"Don't. Set him free and plead ignorance," Bob advised. "Look, why don't I handle it? You go upstairs, I'll join you in a few minutes."

"You're a star, Bob. Thank him for coming in. Keep it light in there so he doesn't suspect anything is wrong."

"I know how to handle him. Go."

Sam trudged along the hallway and up the stairs, her shoulders slumped in defeat. She didn't know why she felt so damned trounced, but she did. It had been a hell of a day, and there was still a while to go yet before she could go home and put her feet up.

She was at the drinks station, fixing everyone a coffee, when Bob entered the incident room. "I'll have one if you're offering."

"Coming right up. How did it go with Lang?"

Bob brushed his hands together and then flopped into his chair. "It was a doddle. The shit won't hit the fan until he tries to contact his bird."

Sam wiped a hand over her face. "That's what's concerning me. What a waste of a couple of hours. I truly thought we were onto something, inviting the two gents in for questioning. Now we have nothing."

"You can say that again, boss," Claire chipped in. "Hart's alibis check out for both dates. I've just spoken to his boss, who was pretty vexed about me ringing him."

"Fuck, we had a right to chase up their accounts. I can't help thinking that I've screwed up these two men's lives for the imminent future. It's true what they say, once they have a record, these individuals are always on our radar."

"Hey, don't go blaming yourself. All you were doing was your job. We had a right to question them. Can you imagine the uproar if we hadn't, and the killer turned out to be either one of them? HQ would have demoted you on the spot."

Sam flicked her head from one side to the other, stretching out the tension knots in the back of her neck. "Ignore me. It's the frustration talking. We're no further forward, and it's driving me nuts now." She delivered Bob his coffee and lingered by his desk.

He lowered his voice so only she could hear. "Stop beating yourself up about this. There's no evidence at our disposal as yet, our hands are tied for now, so what's the point in punishing yourself?"

"Because it makes me feel better."

"You might want to tell your face that, because from where I'm sitting, I think that's a pile of horseshit."

Sam laughed. "I can always count on you putting a smile on my face, one way or another. I'll be in my office."

"You're also dealing with personal crap that's affecting you, and please, don't go denying it. I have a solution, if you want to hear it?"

Sam wagged a finger. "I think I can guess what that is, and it ain't going to happen, Bob Jones. Let the solicitors deal with it."

"I've heard that before. If it's getting you down, you should give me the green light to nip round there and sort him out once and for all."

"I've already told you, that won't be necessary. Thanks for caring, but I'm dealing with it. Let's get back to work, folks. Search for what we're missing."

"Nothing, as far as I can see, we've dealt with everything that has come our way," Bob replied.

"All we've got to go on is the car, the Ford Puma. We need to up our efforts to trace that car."

Bob nodded. "Alex and I will get on it now."

Sam drifted into her office and became engrossed in paperwork for the next couple of hours. At six-fifteen, she sent the rest of the team home. Bob remained behind and walked her out to the car.

"How are you?"

She punched him gently in the arm. "You worry too much, I'm fine."

"You're a friend as well as my boss. If something is concerning you, then it affects me, too. Are you sure you don't want me to go round there and have it out with the tosser?"

"No, leave it. Go home and enjoy the rest of your evening. Give Abigail a hug from me."

"I will. I hope you don't get any more shit from Chris today."

"He wouldn't dare," she said unconvincingly.

She slipped behind her steering wheel and began the drive home. Sam flicked around a few of the radio channels and stopped on one playing one of her favourite songs: *Perfect* by Ed Sheeran. She tapped her fingers and sang along whilst concentrating on the road ahead of her.

Suddenly, the car in front slammed on its brakes, and she smashed into the back of it. Sam sat there for an instant, momentarily dazed, but being the professional she was, she unhooked her seatbelt and jumped out of the car to make sure the driver was okay.

There were two men in the car, both in their mid-twenties. Sam's suspicion gene was on full alert.

"Hi, are you all right?" She glanced at the road ahead. There was nothing there, no animal had been struck, and there wasn't another car in sight.

"Yeah. Crap, didn't you see me apply my brakes?" the driver barked, rubbing at his neck.

Sam slipped her hand into her pocket and removed her warrant card. "DI Cobbs. No, not until it was far too late to avert a crash. Why did you brake?"

The two men stared at her and gulped.

"Don't bother answering that, I know an insurance scam when I come across one. Luckily, I have a camera on board to back up my theory. Hand over your driving licence and your insurance details."

"What the fuck for? You drove into the back of me, lady. Whether you're a copper or not, I'm in the right here."

"We'll see about that." Sam removed her phone from her other pocket and called nine-nine-nine. "Hello, yes, this is DI Sam Cobbs. I've been involved in an RTA, suspected insurance scam. I need immediate assistance at the scene. I'm on the A596 close to the Royal George Inn."

"I'll have a patrol car with you in a few minutes, ma'am,"

the woman at the other end said. "Any injuries to either party?"

"Miraculously not. All fit and well from what I can see."

"Two cars are on the way, ma'am, they should be with you within five minutes."

"I'll wait with the other driver and his passenger. Thanks." Sam ended the call and kept her phone handy just in case the men caused any trouble. "Have you reconsidered your claim yet, Mr Tyler?" she asked, noting the man's name on his driving licence.

"No. You hit me. End of. My claim is an honest and fair one. You're the one in the wrong here, not me, got that?"

"Oh, I understand completely, sir. We'll see what the Accident Investigation Officer has to say, given the evidence I can supply from my camera."

Both men looked at each other and grimaced. Then the driver reached for his key and switched on the car.

"Don't even think about it. You'll be found within half an hour. Drive off now, and any offences you have caused will be doubled."

"Bollocks, I ain't having this."

Sam backed away as the car sped off. She snapped off a picture of the Range Rover's plate number and rang the control centre rather than go through the emergency line. "Yes, this is DI Cobbs, you were sending two patrol cars my way after I collided with an insurance scammer, well… they've just taken off." She read out the licence number.

"It's okay, ma'am. We'll alert all vehicles in the area, they won't get far."

Sam nodded and waved the driving licence she was still holding. "Damn right, they left me a little present. Their ID."

The woman laughed. "Silly people."

"Yep. I'll hang around for ten minutes, if you can hurry

the attending cars up for me. I'm dead on my feet and need to get home."

"I'll chase them up now. Hold the line."

Sam took the opportunity to examine the damage the scammers had caused. It wasn't much, thanks to her quick thinking: a broken headlight and a small dent in the bumper. She would ring her mechanic friend, Gary, and he'd have it sorted within a day or two. She knew he'd loan her a car over the weekend. Luckily, she wasn't on duty either Saturday or Sunday, so there was no need to call on Bob to ferry her around.

"Are you there, DI Cobbs?"

"I'm here."

"Good. They're two minutes away now. I've told them to get a move on."

"Thanks, that's much appreciated. I'll wait in my car."

"Are you sure you're not hurt?"

"Nope, I'm fine. My car, not so. I'm going to end the call now and get onto my mechanic. Thanks for your assistance this evening."

"Take care of yourself."

Sam entered the car and locked herself in. She searched for Gary's number and called him. "Sorry to trouble you, Gary. It's Sam Cobbs, I've got a bit of an emergency."

"Do you need me to come out and pick you up, Sam?"

"No. But I need you to fix my car."

"Oops, had a prang in it, have you?"

"Sort of. An insurance scammer got me."

"Shit. What a pain in the arse. There's been a spate of them trying their sodding luck in the area lately. Do you want to drop it off tomorrow? I'm free late morning. Is it bad?"

"That'd be great. It's not too bad, a busted headlight and a dent in the bumper."

"I should have it done for you ready to pick up tomorrow evening, providing I can get the parts."

"Wonderful."

"I know I am. You tell me often enough."

Sam laughed. "Because it's true. I'll see you in the morning. Oh wait, any chance of a loan car for the day?"

"Yeah, I'll lend you mine, how's that?"

"I suppose it'll have to do. I hope it's been valeted recently and is insured for all drivers."

"It hasn't." He laughed. "Feel free to do it if you get a spare minute or two. See you in the morning, around eight-thirty?"

"I'll be there. Thanks, Gary."

Not long after ending the call, the first of the patrol vehicles arrived. She ran through what had occurred, and the officer took down a statement. Sam hung on to the driver's ID so she could deal with that aspect herself, although she did give the officer the driver's address.

"He probably won't be there. He gave the impression that he was the crafty sort, you know the type, cocky and self-assured."

"All too well, ma'am. We'll haul his arse in when he's least expecting it. Are you okay?"

"Yes, angry more than injured."

He walked around the front of the car and whistled. "Nevertheless, that's going to cost a pretty penny."

"I thought it might. Luckily, I have a great mechanic who always looks after me."

"I'd hang on to him, they're few and far between these days."

"Exactly. Okay, can I be on my way now?"

"Yes, of course. Sorry to hold you up. I'll keep you informed of any progress we make over the next few days."

Sam handed him one of her cards. "Thanks, you can ring me day or night on that number."

"Enjoy the rest of your evening."

"I'll do my best." Sam returned to her car and drove off, hesitantly at first, her nerves jangling, despite taking a few calming breaths. She was driving illegally with only one headlight working and crossed her fingers, hoping she would make it home without further incident.

She drove to within a few streets of her cottage and noticed a familiar van parked in a side street. Her heart sank. *Fuck off, Chris, I'm not in the mood for you tonight.*

He must have seen her arrive because he leapt out of the vehicle and flagged her down. Sam pulled into a gap up ahead, thinking twice, even three times about whether she was doing the right thing, talking to him. She lowered her window an inch.

"Have you had an accident? You've only got one headlight working."

"Stop stating the obvious, Chris. I've had a long, tiring day, and I'm late relieving Doreen of her dog-sitting duties as it is. What do you want?"

"You're a harsh woman, Sam Cobbs."

"You're wasting time. Get on with it," she said, her anger rising.

"I need to know when I'm going to get some money, Sam. It's not too much to ask, is it?"

"And I've told you, more times than I care to mention, it's in the hands of my solicitor. If you're not satisfied with how your solicitor is dealing with things, then I suggest you employ a new one."

He groaned. "Come on, you can do better than that."

"I can't. Have you seen the state of my car? That's going to cost me an arm and a leg to put right. You're earning, aren't you?"

"I told you. Things have dried up since the pandemic

ended, if it has ended, and the cost-of-living crisis is biting me in the bum."

"It's like that for everyone, including me, Chris. I'm on a fixed salary. It's different for you. You shouldn't need me to tell you what to do. You chose to leave me, I didn't kick you out."

He peered over his shoulder at a man walking his dog towards them. "Don't kick off, Sam."

"I'm not. All I'm stating are the facts. Now, if you'll excuse me, I have a hungry dog to pick up, walk and feed before I can even think about making dinner for myself."

"Can't *he* do it?"

She had a rough idea who the *he* was that Chris was referring to but decided to play ignorant all the same. "As much as I love Sonny, I don't think he's clever enough to walk and feed himself, do you?" She suppressed the giggle threatening to materialise.

"Ha bloody ha. You know who I meant, that new fella of yours."

"Actually, Rhys has a late client this evening and won't be home until around eight."

"He's got you where he wants you, hasn't he? Working all the hours and then coming home, doing all the cooking. Does he expect his meals on the table for when he walks through the door?"

The iciness in his tone pissed her off. "I don't have to defend what either of us does, not to you or anyone else for that matter. I… no, I'm not going there. My new relationship has nothing to do with you, you hear me?"

"Ooo… tetchy. Have I touched a nerve, Sam? Spoken the truth and it's only just dawning on you?"

She started the engine and raised her window. He leapt in front of her car and placed his hands on the bonnet. Something about his behaviour caused her concern. She reversed the car and quickly drew away before he had a chance to realise what she was up to. Glancing back in the mirror, she saw him first shake his fist at her and then place his hands on his head and look at the sky, as though regretting his decision to act up. Still, he wasn't her problem any more. He had his own life to lead. He had been the one calling the shots when he'd gone behind her back to start an affair. She had no reason to feel either guilty or remorseful for what she did or said to him now.

CHAPTER 10

Saturday

ANOTHER PLAN WAS HATCHING. Marco had itchy feet and fingers. The only way to get rid of the sensation was to go on the prowl again, in search of yet another victim. He had someone in mind, knew the man concerned would need careful handling. He'd need to come up with something special to capture his next target. A lightbulb went off in his head. He used the landline to make the call. "Hi, Phil, how's it going?"

"Who's this?"

"Doh, it's Marco Owen. I know it's quite early on a Saturday but I was wondering how you're fixed today, mate."

"Oh, hi. I've got a few things on later, a swim with the rest of the club. Are you going today?"

"Yeah, it's out at Wastwater, right?"

"Yep, I've not swum out there for a while. I'm really looking forward to it, it's been a crap week workwise."

"Shame, we all get them, mate. Listen, talking of work, I have a special project I need to take care of for my boss over the weekend, and guess what? The damn computer threw a wobbly this morning and crashed. Any chance you could cast an expert eye over it for me?"

A long, drawn-out silence was followed by a reluctant sigh. "I guess I can. Are you at home?"

"That's right. You know the address, don't you?"

"Yeah, I made a note of it the last time I was there. I could come at around eleven, how does that sound? I'll have to run it past my missus first, like."

Marco winced and almost called it off, but the eagerness to feel another life slip through his fingers again proved too much of a temptation to resist. "Yeah, sounds good to me. I really appreciate this, Phil."

"You can tell me that after I present you with the bill. It's time and a half at the weekends." Phil laughed.

"That figures. See you later. I'll get everything set up and ready for your arrival."

"Sounds perfect. See you soon."

Marco grinned and replaced the phone in its docking station. He then spent the next half an hour tidying up the cottage and ensuring the computer was set up ready for Phil to take a look. He'd make his move not long after Phil arrived. He salivated at the prospect. He knew he was taking a risk, getting the man to come to his home, but it was also cutting a corner in his grand plan as well.

THE DOORBELL RANG at five minutes to eleven. Marco rubbed his hands on his way to answer the front door. He loved it when a target was eager. "Hey, cheers for coming, Phil. I've got everything ready for you. Do you want a coffee?"

"No worries. That's what mates are for, right? Not for me, not long had a full English, and I'm stuffed."

"Okay, it's through here." Marco showed Phil into the lounge, and they sat at the desk in the two chairs Marco had set up.

Phil placed his bag on the floor alongside him and switched on the screen to the computer. It came to life immediately.

"Well, I have no words. I tried everything earlier on, and it was sodding dead."

Phil raised an eyebrow. "It wouldn't hurt to give it the once-over while I'm here. What other problems have you been having lately?"

"A bit temperamental during the start-up and shutdown processes. I thought it might be because it's a few years old. What do you reckon?"

"Let's take a look. How old did you say it was?"

"I didn't. God, now you're asking, you know how time flies. I suppose around five, that's old in computer terms, isn't it? I've kept it updated with the latest software. That should make a difference to how it performs, shouldn't it?"

"It definitely does. Is that offer of a coffee still on the table?"

Marco smiled. "Sure, I'll be back in a mo."

He stepped out of the room, sneaking a peek over his shoulder to see how engrossed Phil was with his task and smiled. *It's going to be a doddle. I'll keep him here for a few days and then do the deed.* He prepared the coffee in the mugs and waited for the water to boil, his gaze drawn to the cricket bat in the corner of the kitchen that he'd inherited from his father. The only decent thing he'd ever done for him in his life. Although, his father had also used it on him when he'd got out of line at the age of fifteen. The vile image of his father beating him with the bat, dozens of times, entered his mind. He winced with every blow he recalled as the anger scorched through him. The kettle switched off, bringing him back from the abyss, and a new impetus developed within him to end Phil's life.

Pouring the hot water into the cup, he added a capsule of sedative along with a splash of milk and a spoonful of sugar, then returned to the lounge. "Here you go. Get that down your neck while it's still hot. How's it going?"

"Fine. It must have been a glitch. The speed seems up to scratch, considering it's an old computer. What I can't understand is why it went dead on you. You did have it plugged in, didn't you?" Phil laughed.

Marco joined in. "Er... I think so. You've got me wondering now. I feel so foolish dragging you all the way out here when there's nothing wrong with the damn thing."

"It doesn't do any harm to give it the once-over now and again. I won't charge you much. Better to be on the safe side, Marco."

"Thanks for understanding."

"Are you going on the swim with the club today?"

"I think so. I haven't quite made my mind up yet. I suppose I have this report hanging over my head. I also have the boss's angry face at the forefront of my mind, looking enraged if I don't get it finished by Monday. You know what evil bastards bosses can be when they want to be."

"Yeah, don't I know it? I wish I had the balls to start out on my own. The truth is, in the current economic crisis, that ain't going to happen any day soon. One month I'm able to stash some funds away, but then one of the large yearly bills comes along to thwart my good intentions. This month it was the car insurance. Can't believe it went up seventy-five quid this year."

"Daylight robbery. Thieving gits. Mine was the same,

around seventy, I think. Makes you wonder where all this is going to end, doesn't it?"

"It does. Still, as my mum says, there are always people worse off than us out there. At least we've got decent jobs and a roof over our heads, eh?" Phil took a sip of his drink.

Marco watched, his pulse rate notching up another level, and the anticipation of what was to come grew with every sip Phil took after the first one.

Phil tweaked the top of his nose. "Bloody head has a mind of its own some days."

"Something wrong, Phil?"

"A damn headache. I've been prone to them in the last few weeks. Gets on my bloody nerves, it does."

"Not great in your business. Have you had your eyes tested recently?"

"Yeah, first thing I did when I started getting them. Still got twenty-twenty vision, so it's a mystery. The doctor is sending me for an MRI scan."

"Shit, that sounds serious. What does he think it might be?"

"I don't know. I was too scared to ask. A mate of mine had a brain tumour when we were at school. He was dead within a couple of weeks of receiving the diagnosis."

"Crap, sorry to hear that, mate."

"Only the good die young, apparently. I've tried my best not to do anything bad in life but failed on a couple of occasions."

"There you go then, that's your theory out the window. You'll be fine. Can I get you a paracetamol? I think I have some stashed away in the medicine cabinet."

"No thanks, I'm not one for taking tablets. Let's see what we've got here. I like your photos. I recognise some of these places from the recent trips we've been on with the club.

Talking of which, did you hear about what happened to Fern Mitchell last week? What a shocker that was."

"I did. Devastating news." The words struggled to get past the bile that had risen in his throat at the mention of her name. He had hated the woman, he'd found her pretentious.

"Not sure what the world is coming to with people bumping off others like that. I liked her, she mentored me with my swimming a few times. Always eager to assist the more novice swimmers in the group. Her experience was second to none, and I was grateful for the kindness she showed me. Are you going to the funeral?" Phil pinched the bridge of his nose again, and his eyelids drooped.

"I doubt it, I couldn't stand the bitch," he said, feeling braver now the sedative was taking effect.

Phil faced him and frowned. "What are you saying?"

"Want me to spell it out for you? She was wicked, masked her evil intent behind her false smiles and the offers of help she dished out. It was all a front. I know, deep down inside, I know what she was really like."

Phil shook his head and cringed. "Damn, I shouldn't have done that. What is the matter with me? Bloody head, I've never had one this bad before."

"It'll be over soon enough."

"What will?" Phil demanded. He took another sip from his drink.

Marco's gaze drifted from Phil to the mug, back to Phil again, and then he tipped his head back and laughed.

"What the fuck is wrong with you, man?" Phil slurred.

"It's not me you have to worry about… well, maybe it is. More to the point, what's wrong with you, man?"

"My head feels like shit. Have you… done something to me? Wait, what the fuck is… going on here? I came to fix your computer… that turns out to be fine anyway, and here… my head. What the hell is wrong with me?"

Marco ran a hand around his chin. "Hmm... let me think. Might I have added a little extra to your drink?"

Phil stared at his mug then picked it up and sniffed the rim. "Like what? Drugs? Have you drugged me? What the fuck for?"

Grinning, Marco ran his finger around his own mug and said teasingly, "Funny that. My coffee seems to taste just fine."

"What's going on?" Phil's words came out slower than ever.

"I'm going to have some fun with you."

Phil shuffled back in his chair and pulled his head away from Marco. "I ain't into all that shit. I like women, man, not into same-sex crap."

Marco covered his face with his hand and sniggered. "That makes two of us. Don't resist, it'll only mean more suffering... for you."

"Resist what?" Phil's eyes were almost at the point of closing now. His mouth contorted uncontrollably as he spoke. His head flopped to the side and then slouched forward onto his chest.

"Phil? Are you awake?"

Nothing. His next victim was out cold. Another wide grin parted Marco's mouth, so wide that his cheeks hurt. He punched the air, elated by the result, and then got to work, tying Phil up. He would keep him safely tucked away for a few days like the others and, depending how well he behaved, Marco would decide when he'd finish him off completely. He'd have fun torturing Phil first, if only for what he'd said about that bitch, Fern. That had really ruffled his feathers.

He pulled Phil from the chair, hoisted him over his shoulder and staggered down the stairs to the cellar.

CHAPTER 11

Throughout her drive into work the following Monday, Sam smiled, reflecting over the wonderful weekend she had experienced with Rhys and their two furry companions. They had gone on several adventures. The weather had been perfect for trips out, to take in some of the tourist sites on offer, now that there were less visitors in the area. Pub lunches, accompanied by their pooches, had been the highlight of the weekend, as well as spending the treasured time together. They laughed, hugged, kissed, all the good things a relationship needed for a wholesome existence. What they didn't do was argue, like she and Chris had done, on an almost daily basis.

Her life had changed for the better since Rhys had walked into her life. She hadn't shared with him the times she had met up with Chris over the past week or so. She could handle her ex. In her mind, there was no need for Rhys to get involved in what was left of her marriage to Chris, which was about to be finalised within a few days.

Rhys was everything Chris wasn't, and she couldn't be more in love. He treated her as his equal, which she valued.

There were too many men in this world who came from the same mould as Chris, who didn't believe women had a mind of their own.

The trouble was, when they'd been living together, she hadn't really seen that unbearable flaw in Chris, but it had been there all the same. Putting into question her detective skills where personal matters were concerned.

Although she was temporarily now over seven hundred quid poorer, thanks to the vile scammers, until her insurers processed her claim, she hadn't allowed the incident to spoil her weekend. Gary had finished fixing her car on the Saturday at three and delivered it back to her at five, once she and Rhys had got home from a day out at Keswick.

She parked the car and entered the station to a very excitable Nick, who had obviously been awaiting her imminent arrival. "Hey, Nick. How's it going?"

"Really well, ma'am. You'll be pleased to know we have two men in custody. They were arrested last night after we were called out to an RTA."

"The insurance scammers?" she asked, wide-eyed.

"That's the ones. Thought you'd like to be told first thing."

"That's made my day. Wait, what about the accident they caused, was the driver okay?"

"He was. He called the police right away, suspecting there was something majorly wrong about the accident. He was right. The constables who attended the scene smelt a rat from the word go. The driver failed to produce his driving licence at the scene, and that's when it clicked with my lads."

Sam opened her purse and removed the licence she'd been keeping safe and slid it across the counter. "I'll leave this with you then, Nick."

They high-fived, and Sam smiled.

"Thrilled they've been caught. I dread to think how many other victims they've scammed."

"I doubt if we'll ever get the true figure out of them. We'll run their names through the system and see if there's a way for us to find out. I hate the thought of them only getting punished for a few crimes if hundreds have been committed."

"Me, too. I've got a great computer asset who could probably help out in her spare time, should you need any assistance. Don't be afraid to give me a shout."

"I'll do that. Thanks, ma'am."

A draught entered the reception area, and Bob joined them. He caught the tail end of their conversation and frowned. "What's this?"

Sam flicked a hand at his chest and pointed to the ceiling. "I'll let you know over a cup of coffee. It's been an eventful weekend."

He groaned. "When isn't it, where you're concerned? It's like you attract trouble just by breathing."

"Sodding cheek. Get upstairs, you miserable git."

They were the first to arrive. Bob fixed the coffee, and she filled him in.

"Bloody hell, I had a strange feeling in my gut something was about to happen to you on the way home on Friday," Bob said. "Never in my wildest dreams did I think you would come out with something like that. I thought you were about to tell me that Chris had been round, causing trouble again."

"Now that you've mentioned it." She took the mug on offer and perched on the edge of a nearby desk.

"No, really? The top award for persistency has to go to him, doesn't it? What did he want?"

"What he always wants, what he's owed from the house. I told him it was out of my hands and to go back and see what his solicitor has to say. We no longer have a say in what goes on, it's down to them. For some reason, he appears to have difficulty grasping that notion."

Bob tutted. "Are you sure you don't want me to have a word with him?"

"No, there's no need. I can handle it if he shows up at the house. What about you, did you have a good weekend?"

"If you call refereeing a full-on verbal war between your other half and a belligerent teenage daughter a great experience… let me assure you, by the time seven came around on Saturday night and the takeaway arrived, we were all exhausted. I shoved my chicken jalfrezi down my neck and within seconds was giving it zzzs on the couch."

"I bet that went down well with Abigail."

"It didn't. I woke up half an hour or so later to find Abigail in the bedroom, crying, then we picked up where the argument with Milly had finished. Roll on next weekend when we're on duty again. It's much easier dealing with hardened criminals than tiptoeing around a teenager and a wife craving for attention all the time."

"I feel for you, it can't be easy living with a hormonal teenager. You and Abigail are okay, though, aren't you?"

"You're not wrong. I think so, although I do find myself wondering if someone up there is intent on punishing me for all the wrongs that I've committed in a former life, you know, prior to saying 'I do'."

Sam chuckled. "More than likely. I'm going to crack on, get the onerous chore out of the way first thing. Let me know when all the team arrive, and we'll have a quick recap and then devise a strategy for our next steps in the investigation." She ventured into her office, the view of the distant mountains drawing her attention for the briefest of moments until she urged herself to get on and start her day in earnest.

She was halfway through reading her emails and sipping at her coffee when Bob rushed into the office. "What's up?"

"We've got another one."

Sam's heart plummeted. "Another dead body?"

"Sorry, no, a missing person. Claire's just spotted it on the system when she started up her computer. She set up some form of alert for this area. I don't know exactly how she managed that, but she's got a hit."

Sam left her desk and joined the others. She walked towards Claire who glanced up, her expression one of grave concern. "What have we got, Claire? Another female swimmer?"

"No, it's a man this time and I'm not sure if he's a swimmer or not yet, but I've been monitoring all the missing person reports within a ten-mile radius of Workington, and this one was sitting on my screen when I booted up the computer."

Sam moved behind the sergeant and peered over her shoulder. "Interesting."

Claire flicked the screen and ran her finger down a list of names. "Here you go. I had a brief idea that I recognised the name. He's a member of Brave Endeavour."

"What are the odds on that, eh? It was a rhetorical question. Shit, get me the details of the report. Who filed it?"

"Erin Murphy, she's Philip Cole's girlfriend. I've got her address here." Claire jotted it down and tore off the scrap piece of paper and handed it to Sam.

"Thanks. Claire, if you're not doing anything urgent right now, I think the desk sergeant is in need of your expertise, he'll fill you in with the details."

Claire's brow furrowed. "Sounds ominous."

"Nothing to worry about. Call it a research job that affects me personally. He'll tell you all about it when you see him."

"Can I grab a coffee first?"

"Yes, do that. I think you're going to need the extra caffeine buzz to assist you." She spun around and bumped into her partner who had snuck up on her. "Give a girl some space to breathe, Bob. We should get on the road."

"If we must."

She handed him the address and issued quick instructions for the rest of the team to up their effort digging for evidence on the two cases that had held their attention prior to their weekend break. "Hopefully we'll be back soon. Don't let the grass grow and all that. Let's get this investigation nailed by the end of the week, if we can."

"You're expecting a lot," Bob complained on the way down the stairs.

"I like to think it's an achievable task I've set them. Negativity has no place on this team, partner."

"Get you. I'm doing my best not to be negative, it ain't easy."

"Granted. Frustrated is the word, right?"

"And some."

THE HOUSE WAS A SEMI-DETACHED, older-style property. Sam reckoned it was likely to have been built in the Edwardian era. Outside, a small walled front garden was neatly filled with late flowering shrubs and plants, nothing fancy, just plants that brightened a dreary October day, with its howling wind and threatening dark clouds.

"Let's see what she has to say." Sam knocked on the door. She had her ID to hand, ready to display.

Seconds later, a young blonde woman greeted them with a half-smile. "Hello. I take it you're the police. Thank you for coming. Someone at the station rang, told me to expect you."

Sam introduced herself and Bob and held up her ID for verification. "We came as soon as we heard. All right if we come in and go over a few details with you?"

"Yes, where are my manners? I'm so sorry." She stood aside and made a sweeping gesture with her arm, then she retreated a few steps once the space got a bit tight in the snug hallway. "We'll go through to the kitchen, there's more room in there."

She led the way into a spacious kitchen-cum-dining room that had clearly only been constructed a little while.

"You have a beautiful home, Erin. Is it all right if I call you Erin?"

"Absolutely. Thank you. We've been renovating this place on and off for the past ten years. It gets a bit draining after a while. Our intentions were good in the beginning, but after living knee-deep in dust and mess, the enthusiasm soon dwindles. The trouble is, once you start on one room, it impacts the whole house, doesn't it? The dust travels, and before long you're living in a building site."

"I agree. I had the same with my cottage. You need to have the right mindset to be a developer. It's different when it's your own home, surrounded by your treasured possessions," Sam stated, aware of what type of pressure renovating the cottage had put on her marriage with Chris.

"Totally. Can I get you a drink before we start?"

"We'll give it a miss, we had one before leaving the station. Thanks all the same."

They all sat at the round dining table at the end of the room, close to the French doors that led out to a pretty patio area full of colourful pots. The kitchen cupboards were painted a rich dark blue, and the worktops were made of oak. Sam admired the couple's taste.

Bob withdrew his notebook and flipped it open to a clean page.

"Why don't you tell us what you know? When did you first realise Phil was missing?" Sam asked.

"Around lunchtime on Saturday. I was at work until one. I expected Phil to be here when I got home. He wasn't."

"When was the last time you had any contact with him?"

"He rang me at work at around ten, told me he was nipping out to see a friend and that he shouldn't be long. I told him not to be late back as we were supposed to be going to the supermarket to do our weekly shop. We were fitting that in before he went swimming with the club."

"What time was he due to meet up with this friend?"

"He was leaving right away."

Sam nodded. "Did he tell you where?"

"No. I rushed the conversation because I was busy, and if I didn't finish all the reports I had on my desk, the boss would have expected me to work longer than I had anticipated."

"And what about the swimming, when was that due to take place?"

"Sometime around three, maybe three-thirty. I'm guilty of switching off when he told me, sorry."

"I'm the same, there's no need to apologise. I'm sure we're all guilty of doing it at some time or another."

"I just feel so bad. I wish I could remember. It could make a difference to you, knowing exact times, couldn't it?"

"Honestly, it's not worth getting yourself worked up into a state about. I'm presuming you tried to call his mobile?"

"On the hour, every hour, and sometimes in between. It doesn't ring out at all. It's dead." A sob caught in her throat, and her eyes closed as if she regretted voicing the final word.

"Please, I know it's easier said than done, but try not to get upset. You've done the right thing by filing the missing person report. What about his car? Did he drive to his destination or go there on foot?"

"He would have taken his car with him, it wasn't here when I got back."

"Can you give us the details? Licence number, make and model, colour maybe?"

"God, now you're asking. It's quite new, and I'm hopeless with the nitty-gritty features. I'm one of those who see a car as a reliance. As long as it has an engine, four wheels and is in running order, it's all good in my book."

"Not to worry, we can make some checks at our end."

"It's a metallic blue, if that helps. That's as good as it gets, I'm afraid."

Sam smiled. "What about his phone number?"

Erin left the table and collected the mobile sitting on the worktop, close to the cooker. "Yes, here it is." She handed her phone to Bob to note down the number.

"I have to ask, what is your relationship like?"

"Very good, most of the time. We all have the odd moment when we need our own space, don't we?"

"We do. You don't think he might have taken off somewhere for a few days' break?"

"No, not at all. We are very open as a couple, share our innermost secrets, so I would have known if he was feeling in the least bit agitated and in need of alone time. We had made plans to do things together over the weekend. On Sunday, we were supposed to be going out for lunch, we'd even booked a table at a gastropub we know in the village up the road. If he was intending to run out on me, why would he do that? Another thing, none of his clothes are missing, I checked."

"That was going to be my next question. When did you report Phil missing?"

"Sunday afternoon. Actually, I rang the station on Saturday, voicing my concerns, and was told I couldn't file a report until Sunday afternoon, so that's what I did. I was expecting someone to come and see me yesterday. I'm a bit miffed they didn't show up."

"I can only apologise. We work with a skeleton staff over the weekends. One of the members of my team was alerted to Phil's disappearance first thing this morning, and we came here right away. I'm glad we caught you at home."

"I called in sick. I know I'm going to get reprimanded by my boss when I go back to work but I couldn't face it this morning. It's not a lie, not really, I feel constantly sick, and I wouldn't be able to keep my mind on my work anyway, so what's the point in going in?"

"Another obvious question, but nevertheless, I have to ask, have you contacted all Phil's friends and relatives to ask if they've either seen him or if he has called them over the weekend?"

"I have. I've rung everyone I can think of, in between trying to get in touch with Phil. No one has either seen or heard from him since last week. His mother is quite old, I didn't want to worry her. She called me on Sunday asking where he was. I had to tell her a white lie, just to protect her."

"I understand. What did you tell her?"

"That Phil had gone away unexpectedly with a couple of friends and he forgot to tell her. She hung up on me, livid that he hadn't told her himself. I hated lying to her but what else could I do? My emotions are shot. It took all I had not to break down over the phone. The last thing I want to do is cause her to worry when there are no conceivable answers to be had."

Bob cleared his throat. Sam gave a brief nod, conscious that he was giving a signal that he wanted to ask a question.

"Does his car have a tracker?" Bob asked.

Erin stared at him blankly. "I wouldn't know. God, now I feel so hopeless. Why didn't I ask? I should know these things, shouldn't I?"

"Please, you're being too hard on yourself. If it didn't come up in conversation, then how are you supposed to know?"

She buried her head in her hands, the emotions surging.

"I feel so inadequate. We've been together nearly ten years, and I can't even tell you what kind of bloody car he drives. It makes me out to be a foolish, selfish partner. I swear I'm not."

"It doesn't. Is there anything else you can tell us?" Sam asked.

"Such as?"

"Has anything been of concern to him lately, either personally or professionally? Sorry, I never asked, what does he do for a living?"

"He's an IT consultant, fixes computers on the side for extra money, otherwise we wouldn't be able to afford the renovations, what with the cost of materials soaring the way they have over the past couple of years since Brexit and Covid hit us."

"All right, I think we have enough to get us started. I have to ask, are you going to be all right?"

"I think so. My sister wanted to come round and sit with me, but I put her off. I think I'm better off on my own. I'd feel suffocated if she was around. If I'm by myself then I can cry at will, I won't have to keep my emotions in check. What will happen next?"

"We'll use the information you've given us and source the calls he made and received on his mobile and go from there. We'll also issue an alert for his vehicle, once we've established what type of car it is

Erin frantically glanced around the room. "Wait, I've just remembered, I have a picture of the car somewhere. I told you my head is a mess." She tore across the other side of the room to a cabinet. On the higher shelf were several framed photos. She returned and thrust the silver frame at Bob. "Can you tell what it is from this?"

Bob examined the photo, and he turned it in different directions. "It looks like a BM—"

"W, yes, you're right, it is. Don't ask me what model it is." She shrugged.

"Don't worry, you've done well to remember to show us the photo," Sam said. "Bob, can you take a snap of it on your phone? Maybe a member of the team will be able to identify what model it is when we get back to the station. Is the car registered in his name with DVLA?"

"Oh yes, silly me."

Bob fired off a number of images of the photo and handed it back to Erin. "We'll get to the bottom of it, don't worry."

"Please do your best to bring him home to me, he's the love of my life. What do they say, you don't appreciate someone until they've gone? I thought that was tosh, until this. Now I realise how true it is. I've been wandering around here all weekend like a five-year-old child lost and bewildered at a funfair."

"I'm sure. Try not to worry too much. I'll be in touch the second I hear something. Why don't you pack a bag, go and stay at a friend's house for the night?"

Erin's mouth twisted from side to side. "What if Phil comes home and finds me gone? No, I'd better stay here, just in case."

"It was only a suggestion. Nevertheless, I think it would be a good idea for you to be with someone, if only to prevent your mind from working overtime. Give it some consideration, at least."

"I will. Thank you again for the kindness you have shown me."

Sam smiled. "We'll get off now. Hopefully I'll be in touch again soon."

Outside the house, Bob mumbled something behind Sam as she made her way towards the car.

"What was that?" she asked across the roof of the vehicle.

"I said I don't hold out much hope of her ever laying eyes on him again."

"Wow, I'm bloody glad you didn't say that in front of her. What's this all about? The negativity you're bloody emitting?"

"I'm being realistic. No harm in that, is there?"

"Your interpretation is totally different to mine. My advice would be to rein it in."

"If you say so. Where to now?"

"We'll drop back to the station, get the ball rolling on the phone information we can gather."

"Should be able to do that pretty swiftly. Claire's usually the one with a handle on that subject."

"We'll leave it to her to work her magic then."

On the drive back, Bob wittered on about this, that and the other, but Sam's mind constantly replayed the conversation she'd had with Erin. It was clear the woman loved Phil and was maybe feeling a touch guilty about him going missing. At least, that's how she was reading the situation. She hoped Phil would be found safely and unharmed, however, a niggling sensation worming around in her gut told her otherwise, but she wasn't about to admit it openly to Bob. Not once he'd declared he was feeling the same.

Claire had worked up a storm by the time they had finally got back to the station. She had the phone records gathered within a matter of hours after getting in touch with an old friend of hers in the relevant department. She presented Sam with the list, in her office, slid it across the desk and stood back. "It's all there. All the calls he made and accepted on Saturday morning."

"Have you had a chance to trace the numbers yet? Or am I guilty of pushing my luck?"

"I'm about to do it now. I thought I'd marry it up with the information we have regarding the members of Brave Endeavour."

Sam winked at her. "That's an excellent idea, Claire. Let me know what you come up with."

"On it now. Should get back to you within twenty minutes, boss."

"Good luck."

Sam busied herself with paperwork until Claire got back to her.

Actually, the efficient sergeant only took five minutes to make the connection. "Here we go, one Marco Owen, he's also on the list of swimmers."

"Fantastic news. I'm on my way now." Sam bolted out of her chair and ordered Bob to join her the second she set foot in the incident room.

"Blimey, we're up and down like a whore's knickers," he said.

Sam suppressed a giggle. "Time is of the essence on this one, matey. Get a move on."

"Dare I ask where we're going?"

"I'll tell you in the car." At that moment, Sam would rather concentrate on getting down the concrete stairs in one piece, having turned an ankle on them the month before.

CHAPTER 12

Sam pulled up outside the remote cottage which was a twenty-five-minute drive from Workington. She admired the view of the surrounding countryside and stepped out of the vehicle. "What a stunning location."

"It's all right, I suppose. A bit too remote for me."

The cottage was charming. The only thing letting it down was the slate roof. Sam felt it was more deserving of a thatched one, which would add yet more character. The only other thing spoiling the cottage, in Sam's opinion, was the prefab garage to the left of the property. It stuck out like a sore thumb.

They entered the small front garden that was disappointingly overgrown and full of nettles, weeds and the odd bramble here and there inching its way over the stone walls.

"This has seen better days," Bob muttered. He rang the bell.

Sam shrugged and prepared to show her ID to the homeowner. It took a while for them to hear or see any sign of life coming from inside. Just when they were about to give up and turn away, a door sounded in the distance.

"At last. Anyone would think this place is a massive mansion or something."

The door opened, and a man in his mid-twenties, clean-shaven, appraised first Bob and then Sam.

"Hello, sir. Are you Marco Owen?" Sam enquired.

He frowned and pulled the door closer behind him. "That's right, and you are?"

Sam thrust her warrant card in his face. "DI Sam Cobbs."

He studied it for a few seconds and then said, "I see. May I ask why you're here today?"

"We're here making enquiries into a missing person case."

"What? Who? To my knowledge, I haven't heard of anyone who has gone missing."

"Philip Cole. Do you recognise the name?"

He laughed and pulled away from the door. "Of course I do. He was here on Saturday. Ah, that's why you're standing at my door, you know that information already, don't you?"

"That's correct. Your name was highlighted in our research. Would you mind if we came in for a chat, Mr Owen?"

He hesitated for the briefest of moments and then thrust the door back, allowing them to enter the tight hallway.

"Come into the lounge. I'm warning you now, I work a lot of hours, so housework isn't at the top of my agenda."

"What do you do?" Sam asked. She followed him into a lounge that swept them back to a forgotten era. Faded flock wallpaper and china plates sitting up on a shelf, adorned the walls. The décor and furnishings belonged to a much older person than someone of Owen's age. *Maybe he's inherited this place and just moved in, hasn't had the funds to bring it forward in time. Not everyone has money to burn these days.*

"I'm an analyst. It's not as glamorous as it sounds."

"And you predominantly work from home?"

"That's right. Started off doing it at the beginning of lockdown and carried on when the world got back to normality. I prefer being here. In effect, I'm my own boss." He laughed. "Maybe I should organise my day better and slot in some housekeeping duties at lunchtime."

Sam cast an eye around the rubbish-strewn room. "Maybe it wouldn't be a bad idea. I take it you live alone, Mr Owen?"

"That's right. No one is likely to take me on if they come out here for a visit and see this mess, are they? Not that I'm that bothered. Most women are only after one thing these days, aren't they?"

Sam raised an eyebrow. "They are? And what might that be, sir?"

"Money."

"If you say so. We were talking about Phil."

"Yes. He came here. Worked a miracle or two on the computer and then left. Top man, always there when you need him. Not that I know him that well. Missing, you say? How?"

"That's what we're trying to establish. What time did he leave?"

Owen pondered the question and tapped a pointed finger against his right cheek. "Now you're asking. We got caught up in conversation about the club we attend and… I suppose it must have been gone one, maybe even one-thirty. Yes, I remember now. I looked at the clock thinking I would see him again in a couple of hours."

"Where?"

"We were due to show up for a swim with the club at Wastwater. Love it there."

"So you were due to meet at Wastwater at around three-thirty?"

"That's correct, except, my bloody car wouldn't start, so I didn't make it. Devastated, I was."

"That's a shame." Sam glanced out of the front room window. "You're pretty remote up here. Did you get your car fixed?"

"Sort of. I had a tinker with it. It eventually started but stalled on me when I took it for a drive. I called a breakdown truck, and they towed me in. The garage is working on it now. Parts are hard to find, the mechanic told me. I've asked him to do his best. I need my car and I can't afford to exchange it for a newer one, not right now."

"Hopefully they'll get it sorted for you soon. Did Phil seem okay while he was here?"

"In what way?"

"Sorry, did he appear agitated at all? Did he mention if he'd noticed anyone following him up here?"

"Christ, is that what you think happened? Someone followed him all the way out here and then abducted him?"

"It was a mere question, sir. At this time, we're unsure what has likely to have happened to him."

"It's terrible to think people can just get abducted willy-nilly these days, without any reason."

Sam did her best to reassure him. "Thankfully, it doesn't happen that often. Okay, you've been most helpful. If Phil should contact you, would you tell him we're looking for him?"

"I'll do that. If he finds his way back here and my car is okay by then, I'll definitely drop him home. God, what if he's out there, concussed or injured? It's not like the weather is being kind to us right now, is it?"

"Good days and bad days, just like it's been throughout the summer. With any luck, he'll show up soon enough. Thanks for speaking with us today."

He walked into the hallway and opened the front door. "You're welcome. Always keen to help the police with an important investigation. I'll keep my eyes and ears open out here."

"That's all we can ask. Thank you."

Back in the car, Sam reversed in the tight road and drove past the cottage. Marco was standing on the doorstep, smiling and waving at them.

"Bloody weirdo," Bob muttered.

"What makes you say that? I found him quite friendly."

"Something didn't sit right with me. You know when you get a sense that someone is saying all the right things to you? Well, that's the impression I got with him."

"You're talking bullshit. I didn't get that impression at all."

"So, what's new? We always differ when this type of thing crops up. Anyway, he's got to be a weirdo to want to live all the way out here on his own. Did you see the state of that place? Made my skin crawl the number of cobwebs I spotted hanging from the ceiling in that lounge. It was even worse in the hallway when I took a peep up the stairwell."

Sam shuddered. "I missed those, thank God."

"I don't mind the cobwebs. What makes me cringe is the thought of the size of the spider spinning such ginormous webs."

"Bugger, can we change the subject?"

"If you insist. What do you want to talk about?"

"The investigation would be good. Any suggestions on where we go from here?"

"Nope, that's why you're the one in charge and not me."

"Thanks for the support, partner."

They managed to get within fifty feet of the station when the call came in. "DI Sam Cobbs, how can I help?"

"Ma'am, it's Nick on the front desk. I wanted you to know straight away that a couple of my lads have spotted Phil Cole's car."

"Excellent news. Where?"

"It was found dumped in a farmer's field on the north side of Workington. They're getting it towed in now."

"Sounds good to me, Nick. We're about five minutes away. I'll grab all the details from you then." She pressed the button on the steering wheel to end the call.

"Ooo... promising," Bob said.

"Let's hope so. I'm going to make sure SOCO go over it thoroughly."

"I'm sure they'll oblige."

SAM SUMMONED the team together and brought them up to date with what had occurred during the previous few hours.

"Seems a bit of a coincidence that chap's car didn't start," Alex mumbled, his arms crossed tightly over his broad chest.

"Not really, considering his location. I bet it occurs more times than he has hot dinners."

"Or dusts his bloody home," Bob added, laughing.

"All right. Let's get cracking. I want you to hit the cameras plus the ANPR, see if we can trace who was driving Phil's car, if he was in the car, or if someone stole the vehicle, leaving him dumped on the side of the road somewhere."

"With due respect, if that had happened, wouldn't he have shown up by now? Either contacted his girlfriend or come in to have reported the crime?" Bob asked.

"Possibly. What if he's concussed or has amnesia, have you considered that?"

"All right, no, I hadn't."

Sam grinned at her partner who left his chair and went over to the drinks station to fix himself a coffee. "I'll have one, if you're asking," Sam shouted.

The rest of the team followed her lead, which pissed Bob off. Sam could tell by the way he began chuntering and chewing the inside of his mouth while he made the drinks.

"Okay, so let's get everyone working on the cameras. I want you all to pick a route leading to that field. There shouldn't be too many, should there? I'm unfamiliar with that area compared to everywhere else."

"A couple of roads at most, boss," Liam announced.

Sam clapped her hands. "Get cracking then, team. I'll gee up SOCO and chase up the PMs on the other cases." She took her coffee into the office and rang Des. "Sorry if I'm interrupting you, it's Sam Cobbs."

"I know who it is, Sam. What's up? And yes, you're always interrupting me when you call, because, unlike you, I'm on the go twenty-four-seven."

Sam groaned. "I'm going to ignore that unnecessary dig. Just to keep you in the loop, we're dealing with yet another missing person case that we believe might be linked to the two murders."

"How do you know this?"

"The MP is Phil Cole, he's a member of the same swimming club the other two victims belonged to."

"Ah, I wasn't aware of this information."

Sam cringed. "Oops, didn't I tell you? My fault, sorry."

"Hmm... so much for keeping me in the loop."

"Umm... any news from the PMs?"

"No, *unlike you,* I brought you up to date on the relevant information, except about the bullet. I really must call my friend. We're still processing the DNA found on the second victim, we should hear back about that any day now. I'll chase it first thing, if I don't hear by the time I leave tonight. How's that?"

"I couldn't ask for more. Thanks. What I forgot to tell you was the missing person's car was found this afternoon, abandoned in a field. Any chance you can get the whip out with the SOCO guys for me?"

"I'm sure they'll get the results back to you in a timely

manner, but yes, just in case, I'll put an urgent reminder in the email I send them."

"Wonderful. Thanks, Des. I'll be in touch if I stumble across anything else."

"Ditto."

Sam ended the call and returned to the incident room, not in the least bit interested in dealing with the untouched paperwork she had set aside earlier in the day.

Bob was behind Liam, viewing the screen over his shoulder.

"Found anything interesting?" Sam asked. She placed one hand on her partner's back and the other one on Liam's shoulder.

"Yep, I was about to call you. We've picked up the car on the ANPR and now we've zeroed in on the CCTV cameras closest to the field. The nearest one is five miles away. We're going back and forth between the two cameras but have come up with this image."

Sam leaned in closer to see a man wearing a hoodie, driving the BMW that had been previously found abandoned. "I take it that's the offender and not Phil Cole?"

"That's what I'm assuming," Bob confirmed.

"Okay, there are no other people in the car. Presumably, Cole is either in the boot or has been dumped elsewhere. We know where the car is heading… to the field. Let's see if we can find out which direction it has come from to get to this location."

"We'll work our way backwards," Bob said.

Sam patted him on the back. "I'll leave that with you. I'm going to give Brenda Cavendish a call." She picked up a nearby phone and dialled the woman's number which she had jotted down in her notebook. It rang three times.

"Hello, Brenda speaking."

"Hi, Brenda, this is DI Sam Cobbs, we met the other day."

"I remember. How is the investigation going?"

"Slowly at the moment. I was after a bit of information from you, if you can spare me a second or two?"

"Go ahead. You know me, I like to help out where I can."

"Great news. Did your club meet up on Saturday?"

"That's right, although I was very disappointed with the turnout. Nevertheless, we had a wonderful time. Why are you asking?"

Sam sighed and prepared herself for revealing the truth. "Unfortunately, we've been informed that another member of your club went missing Saturday afternoon."

Brenda gasped. "No, no, no. Whatever does this mean? Are any of us safe?"

"As I told you the other day, I would prefer it if you all remained vigilant for the time being. Can you tell me if either Phil Cole or Marco Owen joined you at the location?"

"Let me think. No, I don't remember them showing up at all. I'm not surprised about Marco, he's missed quite a few meetings in the past six months. Only last month I had to ring him, ask him if he was committed to the club or not."

"Interesting, and what was his response?"

"He lost his temper with me. Oh dear, something tells me I should have told you about this the other day when we met."

"Possibly. What do you know about him?"

"He's had a rough upbringing from what I could tell. He's been with the club a little over a year. Started off really enthusiastic about swimming and learning from the others, but then his enthusiasm dwindled and he began missing some of the meet-ups. Then when he did show up he became moody and kind of distant from everyone else."

"Okay, that's something we really should have been told about earlier, but not to worry. I'll be in touch should any other questions come to mind."

"I can only apologise for messing up, Inspector, blame the shock ripping through me like a tsunami at the time. I'm sure it alters the mind and how we think."

"Please, don't worry. Stay safe. Maybe it would be best if you don't hold any meetings for now, just for the next couple of weeks."

"That's an excellent idea. I'll cancel the arrangements we've made for this weekend."

"Goodbye, Brenda."

Sam contemplated what to do next. When they had visited Owen earlier, he didn't seem reserved or angry to see them. *Was it all an act? Was he playing us?* She went back to Bob and Liam. "Liam, can you get me a close-up of the driver?"

"Bear with me, I'll see what I can do."

Bob frowned and asked, "Something going on?"

"I've just had an interesting conversation with Brenda. She revealed something that she forgot to mention when we questioned her the other day."

"About?"

"About Marco Owen. He's altered in the last few months, become more reserved, lost his enthusiasm for the club. She had to have a word with him last month about possibly revoking his membership."

"Shit! And I bet she's the type to blame the police when investigations go wrong."

Sam shrugged. "There's nothing we can do about it now, except to focus our efforts on Owen. I'll be right back." She crossed the room. "Claire, I need you to find out what you can about Marco Owen. Suzanna, can you call the garages within a ten-mile radius of his home, see if any of them have dealt with him lately, preferably over the weekend?"

Both ladies got to work. Sam paced the floor, one ear on the conversation Suzanna was having with the garages she had sourced. One garage in particular came up trumps. Suzanna ended the call and gave Sam the notes she'd scribbled down.

"So, the last time he used them was over two months ago, and he's a regular by the look of things. Why did he lie to us?"

"Jesus…"

Sam rushed over to Claire's desk. Her drained face was a picture of concern.

"What's wrong?" Sam asked.

"I took a punt and looked up what type of car Owen drives."

"Fuck, it's not a Ford Puma, is it?"

Claire nodded. "Sorry, I should have checked before."

Sam wagged a finger at the sergeant. "Don't you dare say that." She turned to face the rest of the room. "I've heard enough. The car wasn't there, or so he said. My guess is that it was probably in the garage. What else has he lied to us about? And where the fuck is Phil? Sod it, Bob, let's get over there, now. Liam, Oliver, Alex, you come with us, we'll grab a couple of Tasers on the way out. We haven't got time to arrange for an ART to join us. Suzanna and Claire, can you take over searching through the CCTV footage? I specifically want to know how he dumped the car and then got back to the cottage. What are we talking, Bob, twenty to twenty-five minutes' drive?"

"If not more. He might have dumped the body on the way, so that would have added extra time to his journey."

"Granted. Okay, let's get ready to roll, folks. We'll go in two cars."

"I'll drive. I filled up this morning on the way in," Alex offered. He collected his keys from the top drawer of his desk and led the way out of the incident room.

"Keep in touch, ladies," Sam said. "Follow the car to the

fields then take a guesstimate of when it was dumped and search the footage on the road going back, see what you come up with. Ring me when you find anything, keep us in the loop."

"We will," Claire said.

Claire and Suzanna crossed the room to occupy the two seats around Liam's desk.

THE TWO CARS used their sirens and tore along the main road to head out of town towards the cottage. They wouldn't need a warrant, they could go in under a section eighteen. Sam's pulse raced, becoming erratic the closer they got to their destination. She sucked in a deep breath at the top of the lane where the cottage was situated.

"Are you okay? You seem anxious," Bob asked.

"I'm fine, don't go worrying about me."

She put her foot down, but when her mobile rang, she eased off the accelerator again. "DI Sam Cobbs."

"Boss, it's me, Claire."

"You're on speaker. What have you got for us, Claire?"

"We whizzed through the recordings and spotted something interesting."

"Do tell. We're approaching the cottage now so make it quick."

"Sure. We spotted a man wearing a hoodie on the road back from the field. That man was picked up by a Land Rover and dropped off a few miles from the road that leads to Owen's cottage."

"Great stuff. Get that all printed off so I can use it during the interview with the suspect. We'll be back soon, hopefully."

"We'll be thinking of you. Take care."

Sam ended the call and parked the car as soon as the

cottage came into view. "We'll go the rest of the way on foot." She removed her Taser from the glove compartment, and they left the vehicle. The others joined them. Liam had his Taser in hand. This would be the first time he would have reason to use one since he'd passed his training.

Sam offered him some reassuring words. "Just follow my lead. Don't be tempted to shoot too soon, okay?"

"Yes, boss."

"You've got this, mate." Alex gave him a slap on the back.

"I hope so. Cheers, Alex," Liam said.

He seemed apprehensive. Sam would need to keep a close eye on him, not ideal in the circumstances. Still, he needed to learn, and being thrown in at the deep end was the way to go, in her opinion.

"Bob and I will approach the front door. You three scoot around the back, make sure he doesn't try to escape."

The team split up. Sam instructed Bob to knock on the door. She held her Taser in one hand behind her back and did her best to act natural. There was no answer at the door.

Bob raised his finger. "There's shouting round the back."

They bolted down the side alley, past the garage, and found Liam with his Taser out, trained on Owen who was at the bottom of the garden about to jump over the stone wall.

Sam stood next to Liam, her Taser also drawn, ready to fire. "Don't do it, Owen. You won't get very far, not with two of us armed."

Owen sneered, laughed and jumped the wall.

Liam shouted, "Stop where you are or I'll shoot."

Sam ran to the end of the garden, paused long enough to steady herself and fired the Taser. Owen cried out in pain and dropped to his knees. Liam leapt over the wall and, once he was a few feet away from the suspect, Sam released her finger from the trigger, allowing Liam to cuff the suspect. Alex and Oliver rushed past Sam, sprung over the wall and assisted Liam in bringing the suspect back to the house.

"Nice work." Bob smiled.

"We've got him, that's all that counts."

Owen was hurling abuse at the rest of the team. They all came to a stop in front of Sam.

She took a step forward and said, "You were warned to stop, you should have listened. Where's Phil Cole?"

Owen held her gaze for a few seconds and grinned. "Wouldn't you like to know?"

"Put him in the car. Liam, you stay with him. Alex and Oliver, come back and join us, we're going to search the house."

"You won't find him in there, only I know where he is. I'm willing to do a deal with you for a lesser charge on the others," Owen shouted over his shoulder.

"It ain't going to happen, Owen. We've got more on you than you think we have. In fact, I've never met a sloppier criminal in all my days on the force."

"That wiped the grin off that smug bastard's face," Bob stated beside her.

"Okay, gloves on, guys, let's see what we can find inside."

Sam led the way through the kitchen, which was surprisingly clean, and up the stairs. At the top, she and Bob took the main bedroom, and Oliver and Alex dipped into the room on the right. Sam and Bob searched either side of the room but found nothing.

They joined Alex and Oliver on the landing, all four of them showing signs of disappointment in their demeanour.

"There are two more rooms up here." Sam opened the first door. It was the bathroom. Again, it was reasonably clean. The other room was locked. Sam searched the top of the doorframe and discovered the key. "Too easy, Owen." She unlocked the door and threw it open. Inside the small box room was a desk and three cork boards with photos plastered all over them. On the one to the far right were the three people connected to the investigation. Fern and Anna had a red cross through their photos and the word DEAD scrawled across their faces. But Phil's still remained intact. "He must be still alive, somewhere," Sam muttered.

"Or Owen hasn't got around to updating his photo yet."

Sam's shoulders slumped at the thought of Owen dumping Phil's body somewhere and them never recovering it. "We'll do a thorough search downstairs. We might find a clue on his computer, in the search history."

"I wouldn't hold my breath," Bob mumbled.

His usual mantra in these circumstances pissed Sam off more than normal. "Will you stop bloody being so damn negative all the time?"

Bob shrugged and stepped back into the hallway. Sam made her way downstairs. At the bottom, she noticed a door close to the kitchen that she hadn't spotted when they'd come in from the garden. There was a padlock on the door.

Again, she swept the top of the doorframe and discovered the key. "He really should change his routine."

Sam unlocked the door and opened it to reveal a cellar. She flicked on the switch at the top of the stairs and tiptoed down the creaking wooden steps, cringing as several cobwebs clung to her hair and face. "Bloody things, I can't stand them."

"This looks promising." Bob followed her closely.

They stopped at the bottom and waited for Alex and Oliver to join them. Sam glanced around the dimly lit area. It was clear of all debris.

Sam pointed out two doors over at the back of the lengthy room. "Let's hope Phil is inside one of them."

The doors weren't locked. The first room contained a

bed. Beside it were a bucket and a tray with a metal plate, some cutlery and a glass on it.

The second door opened, and the stench hit them. "Shit, let's get him out of there."

"Help me, please!" Phil croaked.

Sam rushed forward to untie his hands. "Are you all right?"

"I think so. He's kept me here for days… I think. Heck, I don't know. There are no windows down here, so I have no concept of time. I thought… he threatened he was going to kill me… today. I'm so glad you've found me."

"You're safe. We have him in custody. We'll take you to the hospital. Can you stand?"

"I'm not sure. He's given me a good beating a couple of times."

"All right, the boys will assist you up the stairs. We're not going to bother to call an ambulance, it would take them too long to locate this place. We'll take you to hospital ourselves."

"Thank you." A sob caught in his throat. "I can't wait to see Erin. Did she report me missing?"

"Yes. She's really worried about you. I'll call her on the way, you can have a chat with her. Let's get you out of this shithole first."

She took a step back and allowed Alex and Oliver to finish untying Phil's hands and ankles. They helped him to his feet, but he was unable to stand for more than a few seconds. So Alex turned around, and Bob and Oliver helped Phil onto his back. The men climbed the stairs and after another quick scan of the area, Sam left the cellar and rushed out into the back garden to draw in the fresh air.

"Wait, what was Owen doing out here when you arrived?" she asked Oliver and Alex.

"He had a spade. We think he was either digging something up or burying it. He heard us approach and belted down the bottom of the garden."

"Oliver, show me where he was."

Oliver walked halfway down the garden to a pile of earth at the edge of the lawned area. "We'll get SOCO over here and point this out to them. Who knows what we're going to find in there? I'd rather not disturb it."

EPILOGUE

During the interview, Marco Owen admitted to killing Fern Mitchell and Anna Ritter and also to holding Phil Cole hostage. When asked why, he hitched up his shoulders and said because he wanted to rid the world of perfection.

That revelation had floored Sam. She already knew that Fern and Anna were excellent swimmers, and no doubt envy or even jealousy would have played a role in their deaths, but what about Phil? As far as she was aware, Brenda hadn't singled him out as having great swimming abilities like the others, so why him?

Owen had shrugged and told her that Phil was good at his role of being an exceptional computer whiz, something he had always strived to be.

The whole interview left Sam feeling numb. She had dealt with some of the worst criminals in the UK throughout her career but had never been confronted with one so blasé and with such unimaginative, yet heartless, motives for ending his victims' lives. To be killed just for being good at something was totally beyond her.

The team, all shattered by the end of the day, decided a celebratory drink at the Red Lion across the road was in order before they headed home for the evening.

Sam bought the first round. The team were buoyant enough, all relieved they had found Phil alive. That didn't tend to happen too often, not when there was a serial killer on the loose.

"What plans have you got for this evening?" Bob leaned in to ask.

"Go home, put my feet up with Rhys. I might even stop off at the supermarket on the way home and buy a piece of steak. On second thoughts, that sounds like too much hassle. I think I'll opt for a takeaway instead. You?"

"The same. I'll nip off after this one, leave the guys to it. It's been a heavy few weeks, and my leg has started to ache."

"Heck, I thought it would be fully mended by now. I feel bad for not asking you how it is."

"Don't be. It's fine, a dull ache, nothing more."

Sam downed the last of her glass of wine, gathered her coat and handbag and said farewell to the others.

The night had a definite chill in the air. She'd be grateful to get home and put the heating on. She jumped in the car and set off. Her phone rang a few seconds later. Rhys's name came up on the screen on her dashboard. "Hey, I was about to call you. How are you?"

"Eager to see you. What are we doing about dinner this evening?"

"How about a takeaway?"

"Sounds good to me. Want me to place an order now?"

"How long are you going to be?" Sam asked.

"Fifteen to twenty minutes."

"Make it for an hour. We can take the dogs for a walk when I get back. I won't be long behind you, I might even beat you home. I'm en route now."

"Sounds like you have it all worked out. What do you fancy, apart from me?" Rhys asked.

She laughed. "Indian. A nice chicken korma would go down a treat. There's some white wine open in the fridge."

"I'll get it ordered. Fancy a naan as well?"

"Why not? Sod the diet for a change."

He groaned. "You women and your diets."

"See you later." She chuckled and ended the call. Sam inserted a love song disc and settled back to enjoy the drive home. Thankfully, because it was later than usual, due to her short stop at the pub, there wasn't much on the road at this time of the evening.

Halfway through an Alexander O'Neal song, the music cut out and the phone rang. "DI Sam Cobbs."

"Sam, Sam, it's me, Doreen. He's here."

"Doreen, are you okay? You sound flustered, love. Who's there?"

"Chris. He's here. I wanted to call you to warn you. He seems angry. He got out of the car and staggered to the front door. I think he's drunk. I'm not sure what to do."

"Okay, I'm about five minutes away. Stay in the house. Do not open the door to him or let Sonny out."

"Oh no, I wouldn't do that. He lashed out and broke one of your pots in the garden when he found out you weren't in."

"Stay calm. It'll be okay, sweetheart, don't worry."

"Oh, but I am. I've never seen him in such a state."

"Keep away from the window, Doreen, don't let him see you."

"I think it's too late for that. Oh my, he's coming towards the house."

That was enough for Sam. She switched on the siren and put her foot down. Her heart pounding and her adrenaline pumping through her veins, she weaved in and out of the traffic and cut the siren at the end of the road adjacent to hers.

Sam was relieved to see Chris sitting in his van when she pulled up alongside him. She exited the vehicle and stormed over to the driver's window. It was open a notch. "What the hell are you doing here, Chris?"

"I was desperate to see you, Sam."

"Jesus, how many more times do I have to tell you? It's over between us. I've moved on, you need to do the same."

"I can't. I want to be with you. I know you still love me. Admit it."

A car entered the road. It was Rhys. He parked the other side of Sam and came to stand beside her. "Everything all right here?"

"Fuck off. I'm talking to my wife. This has nothing to do with you."

"You're wrong, Chris, this has everything to do with Rhys, he's my partner now. Our past relationship affects all of us," Sam corrected him. "Go home, I can hear how drunk you are."

"I don't have a home," Chris shouted. "This is my home."

"He can't drive in this state," Rhys pointed out.

"I'm not drunk, I've only had a couple. Are you going to dump him and come back to me, Sam?"

"No. *Never*. Stop asking me and get on with your life, Chris. There's no going back for us, do you hear me?"

"If that's the case, then there's nothing left for me." He reached across to the passenger seat and grabbed a petrol can which he proceeded to pour over his head.

"No! What are you doing, you bloody idiot? Get out of the van," Sam screeched and tugged at the van's door, but it was locked. She peered over her shoulder to see if Doreen was watching—she was. Sam gestured for her to get back.

Doreen took the hint and pulled the curtain across, blocking the view.

"You don't want to do this, Chris. Let's sit down and discuss what's going on." Rhys powered into professional mode.

Sam clung to his arm.

Chris stared at them both, tears welling up in his eyes, probably from the fumes of the petrol. "I need you, Sam. I'm nothing without you. Please, won't you reconsider?"

"I can't. Listen to Rhys, he can get you the help you need to get over this, Chris. Don't do this."

"It's too late…" He flicked the top off a lighter.

Everything else happened so fast… Rhys yanked her backwards as the inside of the van lit up like a bonfire on November the fifth. Chris's screams filled the night air.

Sam finally found her voice and cried out, "No… Chris… No…!"

THE END

THANK you for reading To Punish Them the next thrilling adventure in this series is available here To Entice Them

HAVE you read any of my fast paced other crime thrillers yet? Why not try the first book in the DI Sara Ramsey series No Right to Kill

OR GRAB the first book in the bestselling, award-winning, Justice series here, Cruel Justice.

. . .

Or the first book in the spin-off Justice Again series, Gone In Seconds.

Perhaps you'd prefer to try one of my other police procedural series, the DI Kayli Bright series which begins with The Missing Children.

Or maybe you'd enjoy the DI Sally Parker series set in Norfolk, Wrong Place.

Or my gritty police procedural starring DI Nelson set in Manchester, Torn Apart.

Or maybe you'd like to try one of my successful psychological thrillers She's Gone, I KNOW THE TRUTH or Shattered Lives.

KEEP IN TOUCH WITH M A COMLEY

Pick up a FREE novella by signing up to my newsletter today.
https://BookHip.com/WBRTGW

BookBub
www.bookbub.com/authors/m-a-comley

Blog

http://melcomley.blogspot.com

Why not join my special Facebook group to take part in monthly giveaways.

Readers' Group

Printed in Great Britain
by Amazon

60117179R00131